El Buzo '6

Barbara McKinley Morrison 2014

Dangerous Beginnings

Barbara McKinley Morrison

iUniverse

DANGEROUS BEGINNINGS

Copyright © 2014 Barbara McKinley Morrison.

All rights reserved. No part of this book may be used or reproduced by any means, graphic, electronic, or mechanical, including photocopying, recording, taping or by any information storage retrieval system without the written permission of the publisher except in the case of brief quotations embodied in critical articles and reviews.

This is a work of fiction. All of the characters, names, incidents, organizations, and dialogue in this novel are either the products of the author's imagination or are used fictitiously.

iUniverse books may be ordered through booksellers or by contacting:

iUniverse
1663 Liberty Drive
Bloomington, IN 47403
www.iuniverse.com
1-800-Authors (1-800-288-4677)

Because of the dynamic nature of the Internet, any web addresses or links contained in this book may have changed since publication and may no longer be valid. The views expressed in this work are solely those of the author and do not necessarily reflect the views of the publisher, and the publisher hereby disclaims any responsibility for them.

Any people depicted in stock imagery provided by Thinkstock are models, and such images are being used for illustrative purposes only.
Certain stock imagery © Thinkstock.

ISBN: 978-1-4917-4051-4 (sc)
ISBN: 978-1-4917-4053-8 (hc)
ISBN: 978-1-4917-4052-1 (e)

Printed in the United States of America.

iUniverse rev. date: 07/22/2014

Acknowledgments

The L. P. Fisher Library in Woodstock, New Brunswick, was a sanctuary of reverence for me as a young schoolgirl. Thankfully, I was fortunate to have Miss Close and Miss Smith, two sisters and amazing librarians, there for many years to guide me. They taught me respect, dignity, and awe for books. My world was expanded and opened.

The IODE, for supplying a reading list of ten books for each school grade level and a prize for completing the list. I finished the grade ten list in grade five. Ten books a school term were not enough for me! Thank you, ladies.

My family and friends, who have always been there for me with support and love, despite my unusual lifestyle and quirks. My daughter, Wendy, for supplying the photograph for the cover and suggesting a title.

Thanks to the staff at iUniverse for taking my hand and walking me through this unknown journey to the end.

WHO, IMPACT, RCMP, and Interpol, for continuing the never-ending battle to stop the counterfeit pharmaceutical drug trade and protecting the health of humanity. I thank you.

To the people of Bucerias for making me part of your community and welcoming me into your hearts. My life has been more fulfilled by you and the town. Thank you.

In memory of Harold Bertram Morrison,
"Rex,"
who took me on the great adventure of life, love, and joy.

Rex, Bucerias and I aren't the same without you!

With realization of one's own potential and self-confidence in one's ability, one can build a better world.

—Dalai Lama XIV

Prologue

I was awake, my eyes not yet open. I waited for the ache I still felt in my heart each morning to lessen.

It was cold, so cold in my room. Burrowing down under the quilts, I found a warm spot that my dog, Princess, had left at the foot of the bed. Snuggling my toes in, I prayed to drift into sleep once more.

Damn, it was quiet! Every sound, inside and out, muffled and hushed.

It must have snowed during the night, I realized, and been a heavy fall. As much as I detested the snow and cold, I knew it would be beautiful outside this early in the morning. The branches of the birch trees in the backyard would be weighted down, bowed with the soft snow. The fir and pines on the side of the house would look as if decorated for Christmas in a woodland fairy tale about animals.

My eyes opened; I had to get up. That last glass of wine from the night before told me so.

Running naked down the hall, I grabbed a bath towel and threw it around my shivering shoulders. I sat on the toilet until, safely, I could scurry back to the bedroom.

Princess sat patiently waiting as I dove into thick slacks, socks, turtleneck, and, for good measure, a wool, hip-length coat sweater with huge, deep pockets.

I knew I'd soon find out how magnificent the new snowfall looked. Prin was running back and forth to the door, ready to venture out. Poor baby hated the snow and cold as much as I did but endured it for minutes at a time when necessary. Her short legs let her belly trail in it, and she couldn't walk on the top, even when the snow was crusted.

"In and out," I said, laughing, "that's Prin's motto." Shit, I realized I had laughed aloud.

Hell, maybe today wouldn't be so bad after all, I thought.

"Just wait, Prin, I have to get my boots on and find my gloves. Darn, where did I toss them last night when we came in?"

Prin didn't answer, but I didn't care nor expect her to. At least when I talked to Princess, no one could accuse me of talking to myself.

Opening the door, we were astounded by the splendor. Oh God, not a tire mark, not a footprint, not a mar of any kind on the sun-speckled surface of the snow to spoil the effect. Prin stood and stared as she, too, was in awe of the sight.

"Go girl, go. Be quick. It's damn cold; thank heavens there's no wind."

Prin ventured out about four steps and squatted. I realized I'd have to shovel a walkway to the front door for the mailman.

"Oh, excuse me, the mail person," I said, correcting myself. The lady that delivered the mail each day was one of the nicest people I'd met in three years here. No way would I make her trudge through two feet of snow.

"Just the width of the scoop, Prin, no more and no longer. We won't be out long."

Prin ran back to the door and sat as if to say, "Yeah, okay, Mum, go ahead without me. Do your thing."

"Baby, can't you stay out for a bit with me? Look, I'll throw snowballs!"

Trembling with cold, Prin stayed by the door ignoring the snowball I threw.

Keeping one hand deep in the pocket of my jacket, I let the dog in the house and went to find a shovel. I would accomplish the task alone, as I did most things since becoming a widow.

Chapter 1

Three Years Earlier

My husband and best friend was dead. Was I angry? No. Was I confused? Yes, but mostly just terrified, petrified, and, oh God, so, so afraid.

I couldn't fight my fear of being alone in a place that every second reminded me I now would be facing life on my own. I made the decision to return to Canada, the country of my birth, after many years in a small Mexican village. At least in Canada I would have a daughter, sister, son, and grandchildren. I would not be alone.

I'd forgotten two important things. One, that being alone and being lonely are two entirely different states of mind, body, and heart. Second, if you run away, you have to take yourself with you. With time, I was to learn both these lessons.

The years had flashed quickly by. Cassy, my daughter, and I had good times. We both loved laughing at foolish things when they hit us funny. Most of the time no one else understood what we were finding hilarious enough to make us cross our legs to keep from wetting our jeans. Cassy's husband, Steve, just shook his head in bafflement, not getting it or us.

I was happy with my family and my apartment, don't get me wrong, but I still had the emptiness inside. My friends were my daughter's friends and in-laws. I needed to renew friendships with people my age, who shared similar memories.

I had loved my three years in Canada with my family, but I needed home, sun, familiar surroundings, and life. I needed to get out of the cold and snow and into the sunshine. Bottled liquid vitamin D just wasn't cutting it.

I made a decision. I'd go back! I'd spend next winter in Mexico, returning to the small village of Bucerias. I was going back, back to my home where I'd have old friends and memories.

Ten months later, I waited for West Jet to depart as scheduled. The two-hour wait at the Halifax airport hadn't been so bad, thanks to wireless. Cassy stayed with me until I had to report to my gate, so we got in a couple of smokes outside.

I know, I know, I shouldn't be smoking, but what the hell. I don't have much else to do, and yes, I know, ha-ha, that's a cop-out! I haven't even tried to quit! Anyway, I wasn't just going for a smoke; Prin had to go out several times.

Everyone still calls it the Halifax airport, likely always will, even though in 2007 the name was changed to the Robert L. Stanfield International Airport. Why they chose a premier's name is beyond me. The airport welcomes over three million passengers annually. That morning it had a nearly deserted lounge. Maybe everyone had earlier flights.

During the thirty-eight-kilometre drive from the city, I missed seeing the dragon's head in Miller Lake. When had the large, green dragon's head gone missing? It was a famous landmark, and the flaring nostrils and two large white fangs were a reminder that soon you'd be high. High in the sky, that is, and on your way.

Scout leaders who camped on the island had anchored it there years ago. The camp, built in 1926, had been enjoyed by scout leaders then and scouts now. I wondered why it had not been replaced. Maybe I could find out on the web. That could be an interesting few hours while sitting on the beach with a frosty margarita or bucket of cold beer. I had to remember to put it on my list of things to do when I got around to it.

"Jeez, hope I get one of those round-to-it thingies soon. My list keeps getting longer!" I giggled.

Enough foolish thoughts; I had to think about my trip instead. Important things like what I would order at my favourite beach restaurant for dinner that evening. Mussels? Tequila shrimp? Ohhhhhh, I might have to buy a larger size in jeans if I kept thinking this way.

"I'm leaving on a jet plane—"

Bag checked, customs cleared, bottle of water purchased. Prin and I were just waiting to board.

"All my bags are packed, I'm ready to go—"

The words to the old John Denver song kept running through my head. My trip and vacation were taking off, literally. Oh, I was so excited but also a little anxious at the thought of beginning a new life.

The first leg of the flight went well. Prin was her usual princess self and caused no problem.

The airline was fantastic. After four or five hours of wine, eating, and napping, I gazed down at the land. Alberta, land of oil, beef, cowboys, and so much more. Home to the world-famous Calgary Stampede and home of the XV Olympic Winter Games in 1988, marking the first time that Canada hosted the games. The sixteen-day event transformed the western cow town into a city boasting top-notch sports facilities. All the facilities have remained intact and available for either training or competition.

Calgary is still the Canadian centre of training for winter athletes. It is, as a result, interesting, full of life and history. I'd love to spend some time here and get to know this city better. The layover, however, was only two and a half hours, so my interest would have to wait for another trip.

The airport is one of my favourites, with good sit-down restaurants, fast-food stops, and lots of shops, busy in an unhurried way. It's a pleasant space to spend two to four hours. Most attractive to me, and Princess of course, is the dog exercise area outside! Now how considerate is that? We plan to visit that area several times.

Back on the plane for another four or five hours and then I'd be in Bucerias. Though I knew it would be different after three years, I was so looking forward to that first blast of hot air that hits you in the chest like a five-pound cannonball when you step out of the plane. I'd put a change of clothing in my carry-on so I'd be ready. Yes, I was ready, more than ready, for whatever the next five months would bring.

"Here we go, we're landing! Soon we'll be able to pee."

Shit, I'd said that out loud. I looked at the man seated beside me, and the look on his face was enough to send me into fits of laughter, but I turned away and pretended to look for something in my bag. Darn, I'll have to be more careful. I'm so used to speaking to Prin, I forget I'm talking out loud. I've never spoken to her like a dog, more like a child of two or three years, and sometimes people don't realize I'm chatting to her.

He'd have a funny story to tell his wife about the crazy lady on the plane who thought he'd have to pee. I'd love to be a mouse in the corner to overhear that conversation.

We landed without a bump, and as I looked out the window, I felt a chill with goose bumps running over me! I must be more excited than I thought.

I collected my belongings and put my bag in order. Didn't want to have to look for my papers and carry Prin at the same time. It didn't take me but a couple of minutes because I hadn't loaded down my carry-on.

Chapter 2

Trouble Starts

I wasn't disappointed. Even in shorts and a sun top, I got hit with the cannonball of heat! Taking in deep breaths and holding them, I warmed my lungs and blood and hurried for the baggage pickup.

All bags look alike to me unless they are brightly coloured, and I had tied a pink ribbon to mine so I could see it coming before it got to me. Going for a bag on a turnstile is the same as putting your hand into the middle of a herd of running horses. I always got the handle and ended up being dragged four to six feet farther along the darn thing before I could manage to swing it off.

I saw the pink ribbon coming that I used to identify my bag and got in position to catch it when a man's hand shot out and neatly swung my bag to the floor. I turned to say thanks, and he started walking away with it.

"Hey." I grabbed his arm, spinning him around. "What the … That's my bag, you … you …"

"I don't think so, lady. It's mine."

"Look, I'm sure a handsome man like you doesn't tie a bright neon-pink ribbon on his suitcase." Oh for god's sake, did I just call him handsome? The stupid jerk.

We both had a grip on the handle. No way in hell was I letting go. By now we had acquired a small audience, and I waved to a security guard. The jerk quickly relinquished his hold on my bag when the guard asked what was going on.

We both were talking, and the guard was having difficulty trying to sort through two conversations in English at the same time. I switched to Spanglish (my extremely bad Spanish) and got the message across.

"Look, here is my passport, and my initials are right there on the bag. S-O-S written on the tag attached to the handle," I quickly explained to the guard.

Turning to the handsome, silver-haired jerk, I spoke in the most intimidating voice I could muster. "I'm sorry, I don't know what your name is, but mine is Susan O'Brien Shaw. That's what the initials S-O-S mean. So I suggest, unless you want to spend your vacation in flowered shorts, sun tops, women's pants, and bras, we open the suitcase. Then I think you'll want to wait and find your bag in the next load to come down the chute. This one is mine."

He shook his head no and said to forgive him. He must have been mistaken. I quickly turned and started to wheel my suitcase over to the lineup for immigration. As I glanced back, he was nowhere in sight. Ha, thief and fast getaway artist!

"Darn, Prin, the first really good-looking man my age I've seen for years, and of course he'd be a jerk. Why would he want to steal my bag? A big bright-pink bow, really? I don't think so. No way had he believed that was his bag! He's only a thief looking for jewellery or cash likely."

Everything went as smooth as silk. I danced through customs with a green light (hip hip hooray) and found Hugo, my longtime friend and, this year, my landlord, waiting for me, waving like crazy. I found myself engulfed in a bear hug. He flung Spanish at me so fast I couldn't have caught it if it had been a basketball. Laughing, I pulled back.

Hugo hadn't changed one bit in the three years since I had last seen him. Taller than most Mexicans, he was muscular and always was moving something—his knees, feet, head. He couldn't be still. He even talked with his hands and arms waving around. I'd witnessed two or three bottles of beer or glasses of drinks knocked off bars while he was explaining something to someone. He still was wearing his hair short, but not a grey strand did I spot.

"Hugo, por favor, slow down. After three years, my Spanish is rusty, and your English has improved, and yes, I'm glad to see you too and be home again after so long! Let's get out of here. This is Princess, Hugo, but call her Prin. I'll take her outside for the bathroom and have a smoke, and then I've got a story to tell you."

"Well, hola, Prin. Welcome to Mexico. I'll put your things in the car, Sue; you tend to your dog. It won't take us long to get to Bucerias. We'll have time to talk though."

Hugo walked away, and I knew that during the forty-five minute drive to Bucerias, he would catch me up on news of the town and folks. He was a dear old thing, and we had known him our entire time in Mexico. Thanks to Facebook, I would recognize most of the kids, even though some had turned into young men and women while I was gone.

First, I told him the story about the silver-haired man who tried to steal my suitcase. After hearing about the incident, Hugo was surprised, saying that the airport is very secure with few thefts reported. He was amazed that someone could even get into the baggage pickup area unless he or she was a passenger on a flight that had luggage coming in.

"Well, someone found out how. Of course, I don't know that he wasn't a passenger," I answered, laughing.

"I can't believe all the new buildings and lanes in the road, Hugo! I knew things had changed—I've been in touch with a few friends—but this is much more than I expected."

"Wait until you see Puerto Vallarta, Sue. Bucerias has not changed as much as you think, but PV, wow, it now is huge. Oh, there is a new Walmart and Mega near us also. You won't have far to go for supplies."

"I'll be happier to find that my little *carniceria* and corner store are still there. You know I like to buy locally. I can hardly wait to get to the Sunday farm market. I'll get everything I need at the corner store, even my beer and smokes, until Sunday. The carniceria always had more tender meat than the big stores anyway."

"You'll be one of the few then," Hugo stated, laughing at me. "Sue, everyone goes to Walmart and Costco now. Here we are at the apartment house already. The trip didn't take as long as I thought. We missed all the dinnertime traffic. Come on, Sue, I put you in the first-floor bachelor for now. I'll switch you to a bigger one-bedroom as soon as one becomes available."

"The town doesn't seem changed that much from what I could see on the drive, but we didn't come down the main street. I'll be okay. You go on home, Hugo. You're missing dinner with your friend. I just want to settle Prin in and go out to eat. Thanks for picking us up and bringing the key. See you in the morning. Knowing you, it will be bright and early. Give my best to your amigo, Hugo, and thanks again."

Until Hugo got down the street to the corner, I could hardly stand it. One last wave. I checked to see how he and my friend Syl had stocked the fridge. All I needed for morning—juice, coffee, and milk—was there.

I unpacked Prin's food for her breakfast and added that to the fridge supply. Believe me, it didn't take long, and, after snapping on her leash, we were out the door and down the street.

"Oh, Prin, just feel that glorious heat. I hope you can manage it without having to get a haircut! You are so pretty, my good sweet girl."

Prin was very happy to squat and relieve herself, and I knew from the way she sniffed around that she was going to do okay and fit in.

Chapter 3

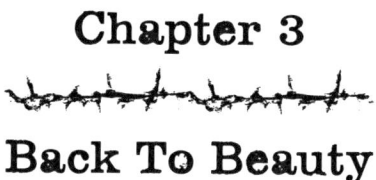

Back To Beauty

The walk to the beach took only a minute, but I had chosen the street and took the three-minute walk to my favourite beach restaurant. Giving Prin time to smell the road, I wondered if dog smells were in different languages or if she could smell in Spanish.

Entering the restaurant, I was surprised to see my favourite table vacant and made a beeline for it. Sunday is still a very busy day and evening, I noted. Many locals choose Sunday as their getaway day and head for the ocean and beach. There is no better way to spend the day than at the uninterrupted, thirty-eight-kilometre stretch of beach here. Lots of room with tables, umbrellas, chairs for family gatherings, and safe, shallow water for the children.

A sign on my old table, printed in pencil, said, "Reserved for an old friend." I understood why such a good table was still vacant. I was expected. Nancy had of course seen to that! I was disappointed not to get a hug from my friend, but she had left for the day.

Everyone seemed delighted to see me again and had many questions about Canada and what I had been doing for the past three years. After many offers of "welcome back" drinks, I decided to accept a glass of wine, knowing it would go well with my *mejillones al ajo, mantequilla, vino blanco, y pan cruijient*. Ha … ordered without a hitch: mussels with garlic, butter, white wine, and crusty bread. Not all my Spanish had vanished, especially the words for food. It was wonderful and delicious, and the warm welcome back was the icing on the cake. My heart and stomach were full.

Other customers on the floor and beach needed attention, so while the boys, men now, were busy doing their jobs, I looked out over the water and the view that was still my preference.

It was dusk, and the sun was setting. Never can you tire of the sunsets. Each evening it is diverse, never the same colours, never the same reflections on the ocean, and always moving with the seasons.

The reflections this night were pinkish purple on the ocean's surface, absolutely perfect for the first night sunset photo I took. My plan was to have a file of sunset photos of each night. That way, I could keep track of the movement while here.

Prin and I left, walking down the beach to enjoy the beauty and see what changes in businesses had taken place over the years. When the golden globe dipped his colourful head into the ocean to end the day, we left the beach in near darkness and walked up the street to the town plaza. So much had changed. I knew it had. Following the news and photos on Facebook had prepared me. I was still amazed as I took in the beautiful new diver sculpture, arches, and trees. I had to admit it was an improvement, but not my memory of the town plaza. Now I had a new memory to add.

It was still a very busy place with vendors, children playing, and people entering or leaving the church. Different Mexican songs blared from many places. I was surprised to hear the church clock in the tower chime the tenth hour. No wonder I felt tired. After the trip, excitement, walk, wine, and food, I was ready for bed. I headed back to my apartment.

Looking through my huge, cluttered bag for the key, I suddenly realized the door wasn't closed completely.

"I know darn well I locked the door, Prin!" I said to her in a loud voice, hoping to signal anyone still around.

I pushed the door open. "What the f … Shit, shit."

The room was a shambles. Everything was tossed and the suitcase dumped, computer case too. I immediately checked what few valuables

I had and found nothing missing. Of course I still had everything important in my bag, as thankfully I hadn't taken the time to dump it out. It must have been kids looking for cash. I'd tell Hugo in the morning and get my lock reinforced.

After checking my laptop to make sure it hadn't been damaged in the fall, I dashed a quick e-mail off to my daughter to let her know I was here safe and sound. I'd been in such a happy rush before, I'd forgotten. I hoped she wasn't worried. She was used to me and my ways, so she'd be fine.

"Let's get to bed. I'll clean up in the morning with a cup of coffee and a smoke. I'm too tired to tackle this work tonight, Prin."

But once we were in bed, I wondered, *Has the town changed this much, and why wasn't anything taken?* Never had my home been broken into before, and break-ins had never occurred very often in this quiet town. Prin curled up next to me and snuggled in for some petting. Her eyes closed within minutes, and so did mine.

The next morning, after speaking with Hugo, I sorted things out and put everything away. While we chatted over a cup of coffee, Hugo said he thought I should call the police and report the break-in, but I said it wasn't necessary; nothing had been taken.

With my new lock installed and starving by this time, I headed for the beach to have breakfast, go exploring, and maybe shop for some basic supplies. I didn't want to miss a minute of my first day in the magnificent sun. Of course, the days to come would be busy with visits to friends, but for now, on my first day, some time alone to soak every sensation into my being was all I wanted.

The next few days flew by, with many holas to friends and visits. It was great to be back, and the incident of my tossed room was forgotten in the happiness of getting into a routine. Early morning walk on the beach, breakfast, cleaning up the apartment, and grooming Prin all took time.

I had to have a vet clip about ten inches of hair off Princess, but she still was my pretty Prin. Those darn little burdocks had gotten stuck all over her. The previous Sunday, after our visit to the farm market, it took nearly three hours to comb and cut the little things out from between the pads of her feet and her long hair. She was fitting in very well and loved it here as much as I did. Well, except for the swimming. I hadn't been able to convince her that was a good way to cool off. She liked walking and running in the ocean as long as her face stayed dry, becoming very ticked off when I went swimming as she was left on the beach. Tad, the waiter, kept an eye on her for me, and I knew she was safe there, sitting in her beach chair with an ice cube. She always wanted to be in the shade, and that was fine with me. The last thing either of us needed was a sunburn.

Walking back to the apartment one evening after a marvellous whole red snapper grilled to perfection, I felt a chill run over my body. I could hear my mum's voice saying, "Someone just walked over your grave." She always had a saying for everything.

I felt a tug on my shoulder and my bag abruptly snatched from me. It was so sudden I didn't have time to even yell. I stood trembling for a moment.

The kid ran off so fast I had no chance to give chase, and Prin was upset, barking her fool head off. Thank heavens I had her on a leash or she would have run after the boy. He was a cute little tyke, thin, barefoot, and I would recognize him if I spotted him on the beach. Well, he likely could use the few pesos; he had looked hungry. Thank goodness I knew enough not to keep anything except a few pesos in my bag. It was only a beach bag and not expensive or important after all!

Then I suddenly realized I had thrown in my wallet just before leaving the house. Damn, my credit card was in there and more pesos than I'd thought. Now I'd have to go through the crappy process of phoning, cancelling my credit card, and not having one until the replacement came.

"Let's go to bed, Prin. This beautiful day just got the shit kicked out of it."

I was about to turn off the lights when a small rap sounded on my door.

"Don't bark, Prin, it's late; people are sleeping."

I opened the door and there stood my little bedraggled thief with a tough smirk on his face, holding out my bag to me. "Gringa, you want bag? Gimme twenty dollars."

"How can I give you money when you have all my pesos in my bag?"

He drooped and then looked up at me sheepishly. "I no thief. Here, take money from bag."

I accepted the held-out bag and, looking through it, found everything rumpled but all there. I took two hundred pesos out and held it. "What's your name?"

"I called Rat."

Kneeling down in front of him, and holding the two hundred pesos so he could see it, I said, "That is an unusual name for a boy! Why are you called Rat?"

"I am Francisco Perez Alonso!" He stuck his thin, bony chest out with pride.

"That is an honourable name, so why are you called Rat?" I asked again.

"I live in dump, find good treasures. I smart."

"Okay, Francisco, one more question and then you can have the pesos. Come in."

Astonishment rounded his huge eyes. "You crazy, gringa? You askin' me in your casa?"

Laughing, I stepped aside. "Yes, I am. It's not my real house. I only rent this small apartment. Your English is very good. Did you learn in school?"

"Umm, I no go school; she cost money. Someday I go after I sell on beach for touristas an' make much money," he smirked.

"Sit."

Down went both Francisco and Prin. I laughed at both of them sitting there looking up expectantly at me.

"Do you want a Coke?"

"Sure thing, lady. What your name is?"

I went to the fridge and got out a cold Coke. "My name is Susan O'Brien Shaw, but you can call me Sue. Now tell me why you snatched my bag and didn't take anything. Then brought it back to me for twenty dollars."

"Okeydoke, you call me Rat. Some loco gringo said I get twenty dollars when I get him bag. So I took. He bad gringo, no pay money. Just look inside and threw it down and tol' me get rid of it. So he not want an' not give me my money. I give to you for twenty dollars."

"You are an honest boy, Francisco. Your father will be proud of you."

"You call me Rat, no like Francisco. No have Papa or Mama. No one but me now."

"I'm so sorry. Is that why you can't go to school?"

"Yep, no money. School she cost many pesos."

"Okay, here is your twenty dollars, but tell me what this loco gringo looked like, please."

"He *gordo*, no *pelo y viejo*. He talk funny, no Americano."

"Okay, Francisco, ah, Rat, here is the money. You are my good friend now, right? Get some food with this. Don't buy junk food."

I barely had the last word out of my mouth and he was gone as fast as a little gazelle.

Jeez, what a sweet, sad boy. Every cent would likely go for junk food.

I had no way of knowing if he told the truth or had found an easy way legally to get twenty bucks, but for some reason I believed the tyke. He was so full of pride. Hmm, an older man, fat, bald, and with an accent; he sounded like something out of an old Pink Panther movie. I certainly didn't know anyone fitting that description and couldn't remember anyone like that in my walks, but he must have been watching me to know where I'd be and lived. That thought was somewhat creepy. I'd keep my eyes open for sure.

Chapter 4

The Jerk Reappears

"Well, hello, Miss SOS. It's nice to see you again."

I was dozy from the hot sun. The happy-hour cold drinks on the beach had gone down too easily. Out of the blue, the jerk with silver hair from the airport was standing over me. Startled, I stood and started backing away! As good looking as he was, I knew he was a thief.

"What do you want? Who are you?" I asked, trying my best not to sound frightened of him.

"Don't be afraid of me, Susan," he said, laughing.

"Susan? Uh, how do you know my n-na-name?" Taken completely off guard, my childhood stammer was back. Oh darn, I'd forgotten he had an accent, sounded Italian.

"You told me at the airport, Susan O'Brien Shaw. Don't you remember when you thought I was stealing your bag? I heard your friend who picked you up say you were driving up to Bucerias, so I thought I'd come up and see for myself what a charming old village looked like. PV is quite a big city, not what I was expecting for a relaxing holiday."

I just stood there staring like an idiot. I was tongue-tied and couldn't utter a word.

"Sorry if I startled you. Let me introduce myself. My name is

Stefano Orlando Sorrentino; no lie, SOS. Now you see why I thought your bag was for me?"

Suddenly, out of nowhere, Francisco appeared between us looking like a little pit bull ready for the attack.

"Amiga, this shitty gringo bother you?"

"Francisco, don't use that kind of language. It's not nice." Shit, where had that come from? I say that all the time instead of swearing. Swearing is taking the Lord's name in vain, which I try not to do. Shit, now what?

"No, Rat, um, Francisco. This is a man I met at the airport, and he is just leaving. He stopped to say hello."

I gave Stefano—if that was his real name—a dirty look, and he stepped closer.

"Okay, Miss Shaw, have it your way. I will leave now, but I need to speak with you concerning some strange events you have encountered. I'll meet you here at the Lobster House for dinner tonight and explain some things, if you'd be so kind. You may even bring your little knight in shining armour to dine with us if you so please. You'll feel more protected." He laughed.

I turned to glance at Rat, and when I looked up, Silver Hair had disappeared completely from sight. Damn, he was good at that. No way in hell I was going to have dinner with that man.

Rat looked angry. "I no like man with silver hair. He talks like big bald man."

"*Ven*, Francisco, let's go to my place. I'll make us a couple of tacos to have for lunch. You're hungry enough for some tacos, aren't you?" I asked Rat, trying not to let the disappointment sound in my voice.

"Si, si, your tacos good. I eat three or four, Sue." Rat started walking faster as he answered.

Well, I thought, *it'll keep my hands busy for a few minutes while I think about this crazy situation.*

Darn, I had planned to eat dinner at the same restaurant tonight too. Brittany Kingery was playing, and I loved the song she had written and recorded. Hearing one of my favourite pieces performed in person would be a true treat. It had become so popular, it was known as "The Bucerias Song," although the name was "Treasures."

I was not going to miss my favourite song. To hell with the silver-haired man. He was not going to spoil my evening for me.

Rat and I strolled slowly back to the apartment house. Softly, I hummed the tune that I so delighted in. Right in the middle of the chorus, I shivered. Someone walked over my grave again. What was going on? Usually that walking on my grave thingy meant a warning. I pay attention to these inner gut feelings, as my intuitive side has a way of coming to the surface at odd times.

Just as we rounded the corner to my street, a car came out of nowhere. I moved the boy away from the street side, thank heavens. The car swerved toward us with increasing speed, one front wheel jumping the curb. Just as quickly it swerved away and turned the corner. We stood there shaking with pounding hearts.

Francisco was the first to speak, mostly yelling curses at the driver long gone.

"Rat, run to the apartment. That was no damn accident! Hurry, we need to get inside now."

I didn't know what the hell was going on, but I knew that car purposely tried to frighten me or run me down, and it had worked. That chill and shiver had been a warning.

The Italian Sorrentino trying to take my suitcase, the break-in the first night, the fat man hiring the boy to steal my bag—now everything was adding up and starting to make sense. Well, what sense I didn't know yet, but the events sure as hell were connected. I needed a drink and a few quiet minutes to think. I was getting frightened for Rat's and my safety if he was going to hang around me. That car had scared me.

I poured a margarita from the jug in the fridge and collapsed on the couch. Rat sat on the floor watching me with eyes the size of saucers.

"Sue, why we scared?"

"Francisco, that car tried to either hurt or scare me. I think it has something to do with the weird things that have been going on. We have to be careful. You stay here tonight. I want to talk to you anyway."

"Okeydoke, Sue. I like here. What we talk about? You gonna make tacos? I want tacos."

"Look, sweetie," I said, explaining everything to him as I put some meat in the micro to heat and got some tacos together. I poured his milk and downed half a glass of margarita at the same time. "You don't have a home, and I don't have a boy. Would you like to live here with me and work for me? I'll pay you," I asked the sweet boy sitting at my feet and swallowing tacos almost whole.

I knew I was taking a chance on this boy. Once you initiate a personal relationship with one of these children, they cling to you and depend on you. I had no choice; by now I loved this kid and wanted him with me.

"Rat works at dump. I no know how do other work. Better I stay at dump."

I tried to reason with him. "Rat, I am your friend, right? I need you to help me. You are a big strong boy and must help your friend."

"Si, si, Sue," he quietly answered after some consideration. "Rat likes you, amiga, but what I do for work?"

"You have to go to school; I'll pay the money. Also you must watch me from a distance to make sure no one else bothers me. You help me with all the plants and flowers, and run errands."

"Okeydoke. Yep, Sue, me guard you good. No like the bad things happen and no like Silver Hair. He bad gringo."

Thank God, he agreed. I thought this should keep him out of harm's way and give him a decent place to sleep. I also thought he was a sharp little street kid and might spot the car and big bald man if around and tell me.

"There is one important thing, Francisco. You must not go near the bad car or bald man if you see them. You must come straight to me, Hugo if he is here, or the police. I'll talk to Hugo and Syl, my friend, explaining everything. Do you promise to stay in the background and report to Hugo or Syl?"

"Si, Sue. I talk to Hugo, but I no talk police."

Princess started to growl and crouched by the door. I peeked out the window between the curtains. There was no one around the door. I tried to open it a couple of inches to glance down the street and a brown envelope fell in through the crack. Picking it up, I carefully opened it. There was no writing on the front. Inside I found a printed note made from words cut from an English newspaper. Holy damn, this was getting scarier by the minute.

"What it say, what it say?" questioned Francisco.

"It says, 'We want the photo tomorrow, or the next time the car will be much, much closer. Leave it in your message box by noon.'"

I was trembling so badly I couldn't speak. Photo, what photo? I didn't have a photo! Good heavens, how could I leave something when I didn't know what the hell they were talking about or what the hell was going on? Who the hell are they? Both Hugo and Syl had wanted me to go to the police. I believed without something, anything except a story, for proof, they wouldn't pay attention. Now I had something. The note would prove this wasn't all in my head.

I now knew it was a photo everyone had been looking for. What I didn't know was why they thought I had it or who was looking for it.

How bizarre this was becoming! Only in grade B movies and comic books were notes composed of cut-out newspaper words.

Okay, enough is enough. I was going to get to the bottom of this, and now they had gotten my dander up. I could be a hard ass when the occasion called for it, and this seemed like one of those occasions.

"Francisco, we are safe until noon tomorrow. We are going to dinner. Silver Hair knows more than he's saying, and he's got some damn explaining to do. Come on. We're going to the store to buy you some clothes to wear to dinner and school. You will be safe in school tomorrow. We'll have dinner, and I'll get to hear 'The Bucerias Song' while that jerk explains some things."

Shoes, runners, socks, underwear, uniform, T-shirts, and jeans should be enough to get us through this. Oh darn, books, pencils, haircut—what else am I forgetting? Doesn't matter, it'll have to do for now. I think to myself, *Sue, this is a child. You know about children. You raised three. Don't be stupid now.*

Returning home, Rat took a shower and put on one of his new outfits. What a difference! He sure was a handsome kid. I decided to put on the dog and dress a little sexy, show a little cleavage but classy. Cleavage was one of those attributes I wasn't endowed with, but at least I could show a bump with a good wire uplift bra. Thank heavens for modern creations. After all, I needed this guy to talk, and what better way to get a man to open up than have a woman flatter him a bit.

At 7:45 p.m. we left the house, feeling safe at least until noon the next day.

Chapter 5

Dinner and Lies

Entering the restaurant, I spotted Silver Hair seated at a table on the balcony, and we walked over and sat.

"Okay, you son of a bitch, you almost killed me. You'd better start talking and now. Tell me what is going on, and what is this photo you want badly enough to harass and threaten me for?"

"Sorry, Susan, but when I dine with a beautiful lady, we eat dinner in a civilized manner first. Afterward we can talk, and I'll explain everything, and I think I can answer all your questions, putting your concerns to rest. I haven't eaten all day, so let's enjoy a nice meal. I'm hungry. You look stunning by the way. Francisco, you are a handsome young man when cleaned up."

"Look, this is not a damn date! I'm upset, angry, and need questions answered! Start talking, Sorrentino, now. By the way, Rat is sweet, and new clothes don't make him more handsome."

Completely ignoring anything I said, he continued speaking as though we were a family out to dinner.

"Crap, might as well play his game."

"What would you enjoy, Susan? Let's have a nice bottle of red wine. Francisco, would you like milk or a Coke?"

Arrogant jerk. Okay, I needed him to talk, and maybe being nice and a little coquettish would work. After all, I had dressed to show my cleavage. I nearly burst out with a giggle but was so angry at this egotistical jerk I managed to contain myself.

Rat said he wanted milk, and Silver Hair called a *mesero* over and ordered for the three of us. I did enjoy the delicious food, as I had forgotten we hadn't eaten anything since the tacos. Well, I hadn't! Rat had eaten my share of them. You'd never know it from the way he now was wolfing down everything put in front of him.

Sorrentino also surprised me with good small talk, interesting and at times funny. Rat was having a great time and acted as if he were taking a shine to Stefano, the little traitor.

While we ate, we listened to the beautiful Bucerias song. I could have written the words the first time I came here. Well, maybe not. I never had the talent to write like that. I so enjoyed the music but was afraid it would put me in a mellow mood, and I needed to keep my anger.

With the table cleared and the music finished, Stefano leaned back in his chair. "Do you want to discuss this in front of Francisco, Susan, or would you prefer we go somewhere private?"

Oh no, you don't get me anywhere alone, I thought. *I may be naïve, but I wasn't born yesterday.*

"Right here is fine, Stefano. Francisco has been with me through every step of this … this … whatever the hell this is. We can talk in front of him. He'll be living with me and doing odd jobs for me to pay for his schooling. What is this photo someone wants by tomorrow at noon? I haven't any photo. Is the photo the reason you tried to take my suitcase, and someone tossed my apartment and tried to run me down? I think you are behind all this crap, Stefano. You tried to steal my suitcase, and don't deny it."

Oh-oh, my stammer was coming back. I stopped talking. After all, a girl spy can't stutter. At least in the books I'd read they didn't.

"Susan, wait. I knew things were happening to you, but I don't know what you are talking about. Run you down?" Sorrentino sounded shocked as he continued. "Listen, let me explain. I'm a retired IMPACT agent here on my first vacation in God only knows how long."

"What is an IMPACT agent? IMPACT, what is that?" I looked and sounded stunned and dumb. *Lord have mercy*, I thought. *My hair isn't even natural blonde.*

"IMPACT stands for International Medical Products Anti-Counterfeiting Taskforce," Stefano answered seriously.

"Wow, that was a mouthful. You mean you're a cop?"

"Not exactly a cop, an agent, but I'm retired."

"Show me some ID then, Stefano!"

He got his wallet and extracted a photo ID card. Good heavens, he was who he said he was. I had been afraid of a government agent.

"Now, Susan, do you see why we need to talk? For some reason drug importers think you have a photo I'm supposed to have. Where is it?" Stefano raised his white eyebrows in question.

"Where is it?" I practically screamed. "I have no idea what you're talking about. I don't have any photo. Look, Stefano, you tried to take my bag at the airport, then my place got tossed, my purse was stolen, and I almost got run over. Start explaining to me what is going on."

"What do you mean? Run over? Tell me about the photo. How do you know about it? I admit I tried to take your suitcase, but I am not responsible for the other things." He did sound sincere and astonished at my accusations.

"A car drove very fast toward us this afternoon, jumped the curb, and came within inches of us. We just got back to the house when someone left this note at my door." I took it from my purse and passed it over to him. "Now I can go to the police, as I have proof, and they'll listen to me."

He glanced up from reading the note. I saw his eyes darken.

Blue suddenly turning to stone-cold deep pits. It scared the hell out of me. I'd never seen anyone turn so quickly.

"No, you will not go to the police. We don't know which of them we can trust. IMPACT heard I was on vacation in Puerto Vallarta and didn't have an agent to get here quickly, so they asked me to come out of retirement for a few days and do some undercover surveillance for them," he answered me in a harsh voice. "The photo is crucial to that work, and I was to pick it up at the airport in a package marked SOS. When I saw your suitcase, I thought you were the carrier for the photo."

His voice softened, and his eyes returned to their natural bright blue. "Susan, I had no idea this would get so far out of hand and involve you. Are you positive you don't have any photo?"

"Well, as far as I know I don't. My bag and apartment were searched and evidently it wasn't found, or I wouldn't have been a target for the car or received that note. By the way, give that note back to me! It's all the proof I have that this isn't all in my head. What is the photo of, do you know?"

"Yes, let me explain. Do you know what the IMPACT agency does?" he questioned, sounding like a schoolteacher. I noticed his English was now nearly perfect and had lost most of its Italian accent.

"No, I've never heard of it, but I suppose it has to do with counterfeiting." There I go again, answering in that dumber-than-a-two-year-old voice.

"Most people haven't heard of us, so that is not surprising. It does have to do with counterfeiting but drugs not money."

"Drugs? Dear Lord, what have you gotten me into? I've never had anything to do with drugs!" I was almost screaming again.

"Not that kind of drugs, Sue. You could get these counterfeit pharmaceutical drugs with a doctor's prescription, in a hospital, or on Internet websites that sell them cheaper. WHO, the World Health Organization, estimates over 25 percent of all pharmaceutical drugs are counterfeit. The market is growing, and profit for the drug lords is over $650 million per year in Mexico alone, not counting Canada and the States. It's even larger in Africa and the Middle East countries, well over $35 billion."

"Good heavens, how can this be? Can't the drugstores and doctors tell the difference?" I was stunned as I asked the question.

"No, the product and packaging are nearly identical to the actual medicines. Some products have no active ingredients and can halt healing, while others are less effective because the ingredient has been cut. Some contain other ingredients that can be deadly." Stefano's voice was gloomy. His eyes saddened as he explained.

"Stop, just stop!" I whispered. "This is too much to process. You mean my meds might not be strong enough for me?"

"That likely would never happen if you buy from a trusted, reputable pharmacist. The greater percentage is distributed over the Internet from bogus companies with websites that sound and look completely legit. You'd think you were ordering from the States, but the sites are shams and usually come out of India or China, somewhere overseas."

"Thank goodness I don't buy online. Have there been deaths?" I asked.

"Yes, mostly in less-developed countries like Africa and China, hundreds, in fact many thousands, but not in the United States or Canada. Only a couple in the past year have been reported from there."

"But why have they started to counterfeit medicine? They seemed to be doing okay with coke and heroin."

"Prescription drugs are cheaper and easier to export and import, and that is why I need the photo. The agency heard a large import was to take place in Puerto Vallarta. They sent me a photo of the shipper, and I need to ID and arrest him before he gets hold of the drugs and has a chance to distribute them."

"I don't think I have any photo, but we can look again. Stefano, I'm so sorry I accused you of being the one who searched my house and tried to run me down!"

He smiled. "Apology accepted. How could you know what was going on? Susan, everything I have told you must be kept secret. No one must know. I certainly shouldn't even have told you, but with you in danger and not knowing why, I felt I had to confide and trust in you."

"You sure as hell can, and that includes Rat. He may come in handy spotting the man and car involved. Let's get out of here and go to my place."

"Oh, that's a better place to finish our talk." Stefano sounded pleased when he accepted.

As we walked the few minutes to my apartment, he continued. "Now let's think. Susan, do you have a computer?"

"Sure, got a laptop. Why?"

"The agent who planted the photo for me would not put it in an obvious place like a suitcase. He'd be smarter than that. They didn't hack your laptop, did they?"

"Not that I'm aware of, but it's password protected, so possibly they didn't have time to try anything with it. It was only out of my sight for a few minutes. Why would you think my computer could help find the photo? Why wouldn't they have taken it if they were short of time?" I questioned.

"I have no answer for that, but I'm sure that must be where it is. Maybe if the agent took the picture and put it in your photo folder, we can see and print it. As soon as we get to your apartment, we'll look. That's where I would have hidden it. Most agents think alike." Stefano sure sounded buoyant.

After getting to the apartment and giving Prin her requested welcome-back hugs, we sat together staring at the laptop while it connected. I put in my passwords and opened the file for photos.

"Good heavens, Stefano, I have over thirteen hundred photos on here, and I'm not very organized. How are we to find it in this mess?"

"I noticed you have the program Picasa. It will let you go to the most recent files visited and also puts things in by date. Try that instead of your folders." Stefano seemed to know a lot about computers. Good looking and smart—way to go, Sue.

"Okay, we've gone through about thirty albums and no new ones added. I guess that idea is down the drain. Any other ideas, Stefano?"

"No, I guess that was kind of a long shot but worth a try. Possibly he sewed it into the lining of something. Get me your bag, laptop case, and anything else you were carrying with lining."

"Damn, Stefano, this is all new stuff, and how will I get my things back home? I can't afford to buy all new ones."

"The agency will cover any damage. This is too important for them not to. Here, Rat, take this knife and neatly cut along the sides of the suitcase while I do the laptop bag. Sue, you feel all along the edges of your purse, turn it wrong-side out, or cut it out if you need to."

After about forty-five minutes with all my things strewn across the floor and table, Stefano sat and put his head back. Deep furrows ran across his forehead, and he looked red in the face. "I give up. There has to be something else. They don't threaten and scare you without reason! They believe you have the photo, and it was to come to me in a case marked SOS. Sweetie, got any wine? Pour us a glass, and we'll talk awhile." He smiled up at me.

"O-okay." Shit, my stutter was back. Did he really say sweetie or was it Susie? Maybe my imagination is playing tricks on me. After all, I am in overload drive from so much information.

Rat had been quiet as a little mouse. He had used the knife Stefano had given him and had done a good job hacking away at my suitcase. Other than that, he had stayed in the background and was not acting like himself at all.

I reached up to the shelf for the wine glasses and bottle, and my tablet came tumbling down. I didn't put it up there and hadn't used it for several nights. I usually send a word game to my son-in-law. It was our way to say hi each day.

Stefano jumped and grabbed it out of my hand. He looked angry. "Why did you hide this, Susan? Did you not want me to know about it?"

"No, no, Stefano. I'd forgotten about it. With all that's been going on, I haven't used it for several days, and I don't remember putting it there. I never keep it there. Rat, were you playing games on it? Did you put it up there?"

"Sure, I played it, Sue, but no remember putting up there," Rat answered in a downtrodden voice.

The poor boy looked like he thought he'd get a beating. He darted behind the couch, and I could tell from the sly look and a quick wink he sent me from behind Stefano's back, he was not telling the truth. For some reason, known only to him, he wanted me to go along. Maybe it was something he wanted to keep just between us. Something had been bothering him all evening. He had hardly said a word and ordinarily chattered like a little chimp.

"It's okay, Rat. I'm just glad we found it now so we can check it too."

Rat jumped over the couch and across the floor and grabbed the tablet. He was gone so quickly into the night neither of us knew what was happening or had noticed the door had been open. Stefano quickly came to his senses and ran out after him. I heard him scream for Rat, and I didn't like the word he used afterward one little bit. What the hell had gotten into those two? Rat had been silent the entire time we had been cutting my baggage looking for the photo, and now Stefano saying words I'd only read in books.

Stefano came back in looking rumpled and angry. "I couldn't find him! Where would he go? You know him!" His voice was rough and harsh.

He grabbed me by the upper arm and roughly turned me to face him. "Let go of my arm! You're hurting me! What has gotten into you, Stefano? I'm sure Rat will come back. As far as I know, he has nowhere else to go."

He released his hold but with a push away from him. I ended up half sitting and half lying on the couch, my shirt twisted, and I was sure my arm was starting to bruise.

"You know him. Where would he go?" He glared down at me.

"Look, Stefano, he's a dump kid. There isn't any place else he'd go. Even the other people living there aren't his friends. Everyone is scrounging for the good stuff. He'll come back here, I'm sure." I rubbed my bruising arm. "What the hell is wrong with you?"

"Forget the drink, Susan, I have things to do. I'll be back in the morning before noon. Stay in until I get here. I'll look in the dump for him. When and if Rat returns tonight, call me at this cell number and I'll come right away. You must understand how important this is after our talk. If the load of drugs gets into Mexico, it could cause a lot of deaths. Don't fool around. Do as I say."

I heard him mutter "the little bastard" as he scribbled a number on my notebook.

Things weren't going well at all, especially in the romance department, and he *had* said sweetie. Guess I'll forget about that department. He wasn't my type anyway. I was just dreaming again. Sweating, but wrung dry emotionally, I decided bed could wait. I was going Googling! One thing I can do well is Google! Searches and research are my thing, and this seemed a perfect topic to explore and get some more information about.

Reading an article I found, written for the International Policy Network, I learned that the problem is worldwide and much more serious than Stefano had made it out to be. Counterfeiting included drugs for treating anaemia, HIV, schizophrenia, malaria, and cancer; flu shots, growth promotion hormone (used in the treatment of HIV); cough syrups; Viagra; and vitamins.

The problem also extends beyond fake pharmaceuticals to medical consumables, such as nonsterile syringes and gauze and even substandard electronic medical equipment. Without reforms, counterfeiters will continue to kill hundreds and thousands of people every year. I read until my eyes would not stay open any longer, and with my mind filled with such atrocities and horrors, I had to turn off the computer.

The mind and body exist as magnificent works of art. Each has a way of not paying attention to the other. I thought I would lie awake forever, my mind filled with thoughts of bodies and death, but instead I fell into a deep sleep immediately.

Chapter 6

I Spy with My Little Eye

Dreaming I was sinking into a hole with no opening for air, I awoke. Holy crap, there was a hand over my mouth. No wonder I couldn't breathe. I started to struggle but heard Rat shushing me.

"Rat, what are you doing? Where did you go, and why did you run off? Why are you hushing me? How did you get in? Turn on the lights."

"Shhh, Sue, be quiet. In dark is better, no lights. Sue, I no like Silver Hair. He is snake. I know many like him from street and dump. You have to believe me; I no lie to you. I love you, Sue. You is my friend."

"You are my friend," I said, correcting his grammar in auto mode. "Yes, Francisco, I am your friend, and I love you too. What happened to make you distrust Stefano? He works for the government to stop bad people."

"Think this is lie. Outside restaurant before dinner I seen him talk to two big, tough men in the dark. He knows them. They slapped him on shoulder like friend. They dress in all black and no have hair. I no like man without hair. I say nothing. I wait. I want to know how he talk to you. He talk bad and push you. I watch. I think all is to get close to you to look for picture so you think you help. I hid tablet so he not look there 'cause we look everywhere so picture must be in tablet, Sue."

Rat had thought this out and acted in a sensible, mature way. He stopped whispering and gazed at me like a tiny spy, or maybe like my knight in shining armour, as Stefano had called him.

"All right, I believe you," I whispered, "There's no window in the bathroom. We'll go in there and check out the tablet. Be quiet, and don't walk in front of a window. You're sure about what you saw, cross your heart?"

"Cross heart and fingers too," he whispered back as we crouched and, in our own home, made our way to the bathroom like two thieves in the night. I glanced up at the clock above the window and could see it was about three thirty.

After closing the door, I folded a towel, laid it across the crack at the bottom, and then switched on the little light over the mirror. We sat on the side of the tub shivering with anticipation while the little tablet connected. I wondered if I was crazy or if the rest of the world was. I was in way over my head and didn't know beans about what I was doing or what was going on.

"Oh, Susie, baby girl, how do you get yourself in these messes?" I heard my husband ask. There was no answer in my head for his silent question.

The tablet lit up with the message: "Swipe to unlock, no password needed." That would have made it easy for someone to use. Dear heavens, why hadn't I put some protection on this thing? I swiped and hit the icon for the camera. I could see the pattern in the floor, but I didn't want to take a picture. I wanted to see the ones on there. How the hell do I do that again? Come on, Sue, think. Now is not the time for "sometimers." Yes, I remember, hit the last photo showing. I was amazed I knew anything about this tablet. It was new, and I hadn't learned how to use it competently.

There it was: a photo of a man disembarking from a small private jet. It looked as if it had been taken with a zoom lens. It was a very grainy black-and-white photo.

"There it is, Rat, what everyone wants. Just a sec and I'll enlarge it so we can see his face. Rat, your head is in the way, move over."

We were still crouched on the tub's edge whispering. Once the photo enlarged, I used editing to despeckle, crop, and enlarge the figure from the waist up. I looked at the photo carefully and all of a sudden knew I had seen this photo, or one like it, somewhere else.

"Wow, my friend, I think we may have just gotten a lucky break. I saw this man's picture in a newspaper gossip rag at the airport in Canada. The paparazzi had caught him on camera when he disembarked.

"Let's see what Google can find out about him for us. Jeez, Rat, listen to this. Interesting. His name is Pablo Diaz. He lives a secluded lifestyle in an elaborate ranch in the mountains. No one knows much about him except he was a billionaire before he turned forty, raised on the streets, became the leader of the gang Los Cráneos Malditos."

"Means the bloody skulls. Rat no want nothing to do with bad gang." He looked very nervous when he spoke.

"Interpol has an interest in his dealings. They know he is dirty and a murderer but can't prove it. The article also says he dislikes his photo taken, and only a few exist. I guess that's why this one is important. They need it to identify him for the deal. So now what do we do? The Bloody Skulls? Damn, just the name of the gang would scare you!"

Jeez, I sounded as nervous as Rat had. What had I gotten us into? I had to come up with some sort of half-ass plan of some kind to try to get us out of this and ensure our safety.

Francisco sat and stared at me. "What you do at noon?"

"I think we'll be smart and pull a fast one on this guy who wants the picture so badly. We'll give it to him but not this one."

"How you do that, Sue? He not knows difference?"

I explained to Rat the plan I had suddenly come up with as I looked at the photo with such poor quality. "I'm going to e-mail this photo to myself, put it on my laptop, and change the man's face a tiny bit. It's a black-and-white picture so will be easier to do than colour. Then I'm going to delete all copies of the original. Rat, look at this man's face and memorize it before it's gone. I'm going to sneak out and get my laptop. Keep the light off until I'm back, okay?"

"Okeydoke, Sue. Be quiet," he whispered, still staring at the photo.

I slipped out the door and got the laptop from the table but couldn't leave without first checking through the curtains at the street. Sure enough, a man was standing, leaning against the streetlight pole across from our building. We had been smart to hide in the bathroom. Now we just had to stay smart, and maybe we would be rid of these guys.

Once I had crawled back to the bathroom, put the towel back at the bottom of the door, and turned the light on, I said to Rat, "Watch an artist at work, Rat. It's been a few years, but I haven't forgotten all my graphic training, at least I hope I haven't. First I'm going to make him a little fatter and shorter. He has a good body shape, and changing it will throw them off. I'll darken his skin just a bit and add a tiny scar to his eyebrow bone." I loaded up Photoshop and went to work. "Done. How's that look, Rat?"

"Sue, you changed him good. Still little bit him but not him!" Rat was amazed at the work.

"Great, thanks. I'll print this and take a photo of it to keep on the tablet. Oh, wait, I have to reverse the despeckle and put in a bit of grain. There, that should do it. It is just about back to the original."

Thank heavens for Wi-Fi. The printer in the living room whirled to print. After it finished, I again sneaked out in the dark and retrieved the photo. On hands and knees, I crawled back to the bathroom and went through the same routine to secure our hideout.

I took a photo with my tablet, checked it, deleted all the other copies and the original, and said to Francisco, "Now we have to get it in the message box before noon. It looks pretty good, but we'll fold it across his face just to make sure it's a bit harder to identify. I'm going to call Stefano and tell him you returned with the tablet. We'll tell him you wanted it for yourself to play games but came back because you had nowhere else to go. I'm going to tell him I looked at the photos and printed off the one of a man I didn't know and certainly wasn't anyone I had photographed. If he wants to check the tablet, the photo will be on there just like the one we printed. Can you understand what we are doing, Rat?"

"Sure, Sue, Rat's smart. I know what going on. You smart too; that's why you friend for me."

"One more thing, we must pretend to still trust and like Stefano. If he thinks we don't, he may not believe us about the photo, okay?"

"Okeydoke, gotcha!" Rat smiled the answer with an evil grin. How he managed it on such a sweet face with those huge eyes and dimples was beyond me.

Chapter 7

Changing Faces

The phone rang several times, and I was just about to end the call when I heard, "Sorrentino."

"Hello, Stefano?' I answered. "It's me, Susan. I wanted to tell you that Francisco came home this morning, and we found a picture of a man on the tablet. I printed it, and I'm going to put it in my message box after we have breakfast. I don't know the man, but it definitely is not a photo I took, so it must be the one everyone is looking for."

Good heavens, Sue, slow down; he's going to know something is wrong if you keep rambling so fast. Come on. Settle down. Act normal. Darn, what the hell is my normal?

"Stefano, did you hear me? Are you there?"

"Yes, Susan, I heard you. I'm surprised he brought back your tablet is all."

"Oh, he just wanted it to play the games, and his instinct was to run with it." Forgive me, Rat. "But like I said, he had nowhere else to go so came home. Are you coming for breakfast and staying to see who comes at noon to get the photo?"

"No, I am busy today. I think you should put the photo in the box, and you and Francisco go to the beach for breakfast. Your holiday is getting spoiled. How about we have dinner there again tonight? I'll meet you close to eight."

"All right, Stefano, that's fine. We'll have breakfast here though, as I have to volunteer at the library for a couple of hours this afternoon, and as soon as we eat, I have to take Francisco for his first day at school. Do you think when they get the photo we'll be safe and I can stop worrying?" My voice quivered with the question.

"Yes, as soon as they have the photo they won't care about you any longer. Is it still on your tablet?"

"Oh yes, I didn't delete it. I thought you'd need to see it so you can spot him before he gets to the drug shipment." Jeez, my acting was getting good.

"Good girl, bring it with you to dinner. See you about eight. Adios." Click.

Well, that was certainly abrupt and to the point. I don't think I fooled Stefano as much as I had hoped to. His voice was off, and he spoke in a wooden manner. At least maybe at dinner I'd be able to tell more. Darn, I hope Rat was completely wrong and mistook what he witnessed. Stefano was the kind of guy I could learn to like as a friend, even though he was serious and pushy. I wanted him to be one of the good guys in the white hat. Just like my old cowboy heroes from the movies of my childhood.

Chapter 8

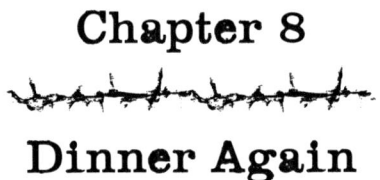

Dinner Again

Francisco was so proud walking into the classroom in his uniform and smart haircut. I have to admit I was quite proud too. The teacher said he would be in fourth class, as he knew his letters and numbers and could read the assignment she had given him, and he had answered all questions correctly. I knew he was a smart kid, but still his knowledge without schooling surprised me. I smiled and waved good-bye, knowing he'd be happy and safe until I picked him up after my shift at the library.

I hurried home and changed into slacks and a matching dark blouse. Plain, simple black is slimming and always sexy. I put the forged photo into my message box and sprinted to the library. I enjoyed my afternoon there each week helping the children with their projects.

When I picked up Rat from school, it was almost time to meet Stefano, so we went to the restaurant, as Rat wanted some time on the beach to watch the vendors work with the tourists. He figured he was learning more tools for his trade.

I ordered a Coke for Rat and watched him watching the vendors. It was fun. They all came up to me of course and wanted me to buy something. I talked to a few of the children. They had such adoring smiles and didn't cram their wares down my throat. I did buy a couple packs of gum, as I knew from Rat these were kids without parents or from alcoholic environments. They all knew my name by now and understood I was helping Rat. Naturally they wanted the same help. Wishing I could take care of each of them was a thought I had to dismiss. I only ordered a couple of drinks; I wanted to be on the ball and thinking straight when I met Stefano. It was difficult to know what might be in store, as he had changed like a chameleon last night and this morning.

Just as the sun was starting to set, I saw him up the beach walking away from us. He must be using the street entrance.

"Come on, Francisco, I think Silver Hair is going in the front way."

As I stood, I noticed the two men he had spoken with were now going to the street also. They definitely were the men Rat had seen. They were tough-looking thugs, dressed in black and bald as new babies. I hoped he hadn't invited them to eat with us. Maybe other agents had come to work with him. Sometimes my imagination runs wild, but then again, I trusted Rat's street instinct. I knew darn well they weren't agents.

"Darn, Rat, run home and put your books in the house and change into jeans so your uniform will be clean for tomorrow. Meet us inside the restaurant. I'll go in now."

I walked up to the road to keep the sand out of my shoes and enter in the front way. I was so concerned with the sand in my shoes, I didn't pay attention to the chill I felt, thinking it was the evening air. Just as I got to the street, I felt a man grab me. I tried kicking, scratching, and managed a pretty good knee to the crotch, but he backhanded me in the face. I felt myself falling backward, cracking my head on something hard and metal.

Chapter 9

Tied Up

Groggy, I forced my eyes open. With gun tape across my mouth and my hands tied together, I forced myself to wake up. Once in a sitting position, I realized my ankles were taped also. I could barely see in the dim lighting but saw enough to know I was on some kind of boat!

Stefano and the two other men watched me. I tried to scream at them, but nothing would escape the tight, wide gun tape. Damn gun tape sticks to anything.

I could not bring to the surface any recollection of travelling or being bound. I certainly must have been out of it for a while. I closed my eyes, hoping that the next time they opened the nightmare would be over.

"Susan, wake up! Come on, stop pretending. I saw you open your eyes. Why did you put a fake photo in your message box for us to pick up? What do you think you're pulling?"

The tape was torn from my mouth, and it felt like some skin on my lips went with it. Tears from anger and discomfort were running down my face, but no way in hell would I make a sound or a whimper. I stopped struggling with the tape that bound my wrists, as I could feel it cutting into my flesh. Shit, shit, shit, I was in trouble, and no one knew where I was. Stupid, stupid, stupid, why hadn't I called the police when Hugo, Nancy, and Syl had begged me to? Someone pulled my head back by my hair, and the pain I experienced made me realize my head had an injury also.

I jerked my head back to relieve the pressure, and my face exploded from a powerful flat-handed slap. It had ploughed right across my jaw. My tongue dripped blood. I had bitten through it on one side. My head was spinning so rapidly I could barely see straight.

Through ringing ears, I heard Stefano yell at one of the men. "What do you think you're doing, asshole? There's no need to be that rough with her. She'll tell us where the photo is without killing her."

Okay, so maybe I was in more frigging trouble than I had even thought. I found him in my line of eyesight.

"So, Stefano, it's you who wants the photo! You really are a son of a bitch. I actually believed all your bull about being an agent." My swollen tongue was jumbling the words, but I knew he understood every word.

"Oh, I used to be an agent, but they don't pay well, and I needed money. This one deal will set me up for life if I can distribute this load of drugs for Señor Pablo."

"Stefano, that is the photo on my tablet." Jeez, was that my voice? I wouldn't have recognized myself if I had not known I was the one trying to speak.

"Sue, sweetie, just tell us how you changed the photo and give us the real one, and you can go home before you're hurt anymore. I'm sorry, but I can't control these men."

"I didn't change it." My voice muffled and slurred, I wasn't sure anyone understood me. "Check my tablet. It's on there."

Crack—another hit on the opposite cheekbone. My chin dropped to my chest. I shook it to clear my mind. What was this, a lesson in turn the other cheek?

"I didn't change it!" Slowly and through clenched teeth and tears, I tried to pronounce each word clearly, hoping for understanding.

"Stefano, please …"

"Susan, there is no sense lying about photoshopping the photo! My partner saw it immediately. Señor Pablo would never have a tattoo! He is too vain and concerned with his looks. I didn't take you for a fool."

The voice was hard and cruel, and even through the pain of my swollen eyes, I could see that it was Stefano speaking.

What tattoo? I hadn't put a tattoo on the man in the photo.

"Not me." My tongue was swelling more, and both cheeks felt like a bus had hit me full in the face. I could hardly speak.

"Maybe guy put on tablet like that." I sounded like Rat, for heaven's sake, but it was the best I could do. I was afraid if I told the truth, I wouldn't be of use to them any longer, and I'd be killed.

"Tape her mouth again!" Stefano was definitely in charge of these monsters, at least trying to be in charge. The big, burly guy slapped the tape over my mouth again and kicked me in the ribs. "Bitch, you're ruining everything!"

Oh hell, I doubled in pain. I'd had broken ribs before and knew one rib or more was broken or cracked after that kick. "Please, guardian angel, don't let it puncture my lung," I pleaded silently to where I thought the sky should be.

The three of them walked away from me, but even with my splitting headache and ringing ears, I could hear them whispering.

"We've got to go talk to Señor Diaz. We've got to make contact soon. That shipment has to be off Captain Chun Lee's boat next week, or we'll lose it." Stefano sounded desperate, and that didn't sound good for me.

"Let me see the photo again; I just remembered something odd. Stefano, as I thought, this is not a tattoo on Señor Pablo's hand. The girl didn't add this. I recognize the symbol as an ink stamp from an exclusive night club in Puerto Vallarta."

Oh, the big gorilla guy could actually talk and think.

"Damn, yes, that sounds more like him. Anywhere he can find young pretty girls to drink and dance with. Let's check it out. I bet he's there every night. We have to find him to get the directions and time to deliver the shipment." Sorrentino was excited.

"I agree," Burly Guy answered.

"Let's leave now. The time is right for him to be there. She'll be okay here for a few hours and can't get off the yacht in her condition. If I don't get to that shipment in time, Señor Pablo will have someone put a damn bullet in the back of my head. He can't stand failure. Turn off the lights."

Ahhh, yacht, I thought. That's why I could feel the up-and-down motion so much. I wasn't on a huge boat, just a yacht. Why this seemed important, I couldn't figure out and couldn't think about it anymore. The pain finally took over, and I blacked out.

Chapter 10

The Rescue

My face was on fire, burning and stinging, but at the same time it felt good, like cool water. I struggled to lift my head and heard Rat say, "Oh, Sue, what men do? I wash your face but it still all blood and swollen."

He tore the tape off my face, and of course, again more pain came with it. I could hear Rat's voice coming from a far distance but knew he was close to me. I could feel his warm breath on my cheek.

"Okay, Sue, I have knife Silver Hair give me at our house. I cut your hands. Put arm over my neck, and I cut feet. Don't stand up; wait for blood to move."

I felt his small hands rubbing my feet and legs. Gradually the feeling came back. I tried to stand and wobbled to a half-kneel with pins and needles numbing my legs and feet.

"Ohhh, 'ave pain!"

"Sue, you hurt in other place else? You have pain somewhere? Not just face?" Rat sounded like he was crying too.

"Ya, p-p-p-ain 'ere." I pointed to my rib cage.

"*Espera un momento!* I fix."

In a couple of minutes I felt something being wrapped around my ribs and tied tightly on my left side. "What is?"

"Sorry, Sue, use new pants," Rat said, chuckling. Well, he still had a sense of humour, so I guess we would be all right. "It not real bandage but help when you move."

"'At, you too s-s-mall 'or me."

My jumbled words must have made some sense as he answered, "Sue, I had birthday; I have twelve years now. Not too small to help. Come slow."

Slow it was, like molasses running up a snowy hillside. We made our way up the six or seven steps, which seemed more like a hundred, onto the deck. The motion was greater here, and I rocked and rolled to the beat. The night air cleared my head some, and I managed to open my eyes to a slit. Rat got us over to the divers' door at the stern.

"Okay, Sue, now we swim a little. Water feel good."

"'At, you k-k-idden?"

"No, Sue, I not kidding. We run away fast. Men come back soon."

Gently my little knight slipped me into the ocean. "Okay?"

"Ya," I answered.

It did feel good on my bruised body. Rat held me up by his new pants in one hand, so my head didn't drown along with the rest of me, and after a few minutes, we stopped. I could see a huge yellow balloon in front of us.

"Come, Sue, must get on banana boat. Mi amigo has come to help us. We get to shore real quiet. No use motor, have paddles."

I put my hand up, grabbing the rope on the handle, but no way could I lift the weight of my body out of the water.

"'an't, 'At, t-t-oo 'igh!" I tried to speak plainer but still couldn't manage more than a jumble.

"Come, Ricki, help Sue. Boat too high for her." Rat called out.

Rat and Ricki, whom I took to be his good friend with the banana boat, got behind me. These two dear small boys pushed, one on each cheek, and after many tries got my butt up and out of the water. Well, there was a Kodak moment missed. There was no way these two kids, as brave as they were, were going to get me up on that thing. It was wet, round, and slippery as hell.

Finally, after much pulling, pushing, and tugging, I was lying across it on my stomach. This was as far as I could move. My ribs were killing me, and the salt water was stinging my face like the iodine my mum used to put on my scrapes when I was little. I wanted to cry, and maybe I was, as I felt warm water on my cheeks.

I felt the banana boat move slowly in the water and began to drift off again, secure in the knowledge that Rat had tied me onto the handles. Boy, I'd been one tied-up girl tonight. The next thing I knew, we were on shore. Rat and Ricki were carrying me like a sack of wet cement toward a small hotel.

"My friend put us in free hotel room so safe tonight. My friend is doctora so she help you."

Rat had some of the best friends I'd ever heard of, and I'd make sure they were all paid back if I lived. Right now, that was not a certainty.

We practically crept on our hands and knees down the beach to the small hotel. I hadn't paid much attention to it on my walks, as it had been there forever. It was not the kind of place tourists stayed, but I knew the bed would be soft and sheets clean. I'd seen the sparkling white bedding on the roof's clothesline.

A woman met us at the door and introduced herself as Doctora Maria. Even with the light behind her, I could make out the dark, thick, wide braid that hung over one shoulder, almost to her waist. She was tall, with beautiful large eyes and long eyelashes. As she helped me into the room, I could see her deep cleavage in the centre of her dark blouse and skin, the colour of perfectly toasted bread. Her whole presence screamed confidence and nobility. This was a beautiful, trustworthy woman.

Thank you, my guardian angel; pain medicine is on the way! I crawled onto the bed, let her do her thing, and instantly was out of this world.

Chapter 11

Meet the Man

Morning, of course, dawned hot and sunny. It shone in the little window, stinging my face and eyes. Rat was asleep on the floor beside my bed. As soon as I stirred, he was on his feet. My eyes opened more; some relief from the medicine subdued the pain in my side, but every bone in my face and body screamed.

"Here, amiga, this help." Rat passed me a hot coffee and two big pills.

"Doc says you take two every four hours, help pain."

I swallowed. "'Ow y-y-ou pay for doctor?" Oh nice, I could form words again if I concentrated and spoke slowly.

"I sneak into house, get new clothes and money. Didn't take much, as Silver Hair might look for you, and I no want him to know I was there. Doctora Maria says she no take money from saviour. You are help to many people."

"You are my a-a-ngel come to life, Rat. I n-n-eed a good, long hot shower. Then I'll dress, and we'll talk."

Don't know how, but he understood every word. My little knight in shining armour!

Doctora Maria came in just then to check me over. She had not been an illusion the night before. Even more statuesque than I recalled, she had high cheekbones and the carriage of an Aztec princess. Her report was good news. Two of my ribs were cracked, and one had a small fracture but definitely would not puncture my lung. Thank God for small miracles. My jaw and face would not take too long to heal, but I'd be a nice shade of blue, black, and then yellow for a few days.

At least I had enough clothes in corresponding colours to be coordinated and certainly wouldn't need any eye makeup. After she gave me her report and showed me the X-ray, she wrapped me in the sheet, and, with Rat's help, the two of them got me to the shower where they had placed a white plastic beach chair so I wouldn't have to stand. Good thing. I couldn't have stood anyway and would have lain on the cold tile floor to get that hot shower. The small mirror in the bathroom cried when I looked in it. I knew it was only steam from the hot running water, but it had a good reason to cry. My jaw and both eyes were black. My bottom lip was cracked, caked with blood. I looked down at my side, and it was black and blue around my ribs on the right side. Boy, they had done a number on me. I wondered if it had been worth it. Yep, I decided, if I had thrown them off the drugs' trail, it had.

Anything I had done to slow down or stop that shipment of counterfeit drugs from entering this country was a good decision, as some lives would be saved. I felt strong and alive for the first time in years.

I stopped patting myself on the back and, with Maria helping me, stepped into heaven. I sat and let the glorious hot water soothe and massage my bruised body.

When the water turned cold, I called to Maria, and when she helped me out, I knew I would live, even though I might not look it.

Chapter 12

Man Search

I could certainly not go out in public for a few days, maybe longer. How was I to find Señor Pablo Diaz, Stefano, or the boat the drugs were to be off-loaded from?

After filling in Maria with more information than Rat had, she said the police were out of the question; they, too, wanted the drug shipment. Millions of dollars were involved, and everyone wanted the fast buck.

Rat knew what Señor Pablo Diaz looked like, so had an advantage over Stefano and his two henchmen. I had to come up with a plan to talk to Diaz, and Rat seemed like the best bet. How could I manage this without putting him in even more danger? I also knew the name of the boat's captain, Captain Lee.

Rat and Ricki came in with hot soup and bread. Oh, the aroma was delicious, and I was starving.

"Doctora Maria say *sola sopa, no comida fuerte.*"

"Rat, it's not important because my mouth and sore tongue wouldn't let me chew anyway. *Sopa es perfecta.*"

I think I pronounced the words well enough to be understandable.

After I slowly spooned the soup into my mouth, with much dribbling down my chin, Rat gave me water and two more pain pills. I felt woozy but needed to talk to him and confirm some things.

"Rat, what day and time is it? How long have we been here?"

"One night and part of day, Sue. Only few more nights before the drugs come off the boat. What we do? Doctora Maria is very worried. Many her people buy cheap drugs and, if they bad, maybe die. She wants to help."

"Okay, Rat, I have a plan. Can you get Doctora Maria here to talk to me now?"

"Si, she waits for you to talk."

My voice was still slurred and didn't sound like me, but I knew I would be understood. The damn pain pills worked like a charm. I had no idea what they were but, hell, who cared? They worked. I closed my eyes for a moment, and when I opened them, a handsome man was staring into them with a look of such kindness I wanted him to lean a little closer to my bruised lips and kiss them softly. His eyes were black, deep, with long sweeping eyelashes any girl would kill for. God, never again would you have to buy mascara. This was a man you'd want to father your children just to inherit the eyelashes. Maybe it was a dream. I closed my eyes again, and when I opened them, Doctora Maria was in front of me.

"Maria, I saw a man, a handsome man with beautiful eyes. I wanted him to kiss me. Maybe my pills are too strong!"

Just then, a face leaned into mine, and a soft kiss moistened my parched, sore lips. Oh, sweet heaven, my dreams were now coming true.

Maria laughed. "Sue, this is my brother, Miguel. He is going to help us. He works for the government and has a free medical clinic and also is a doctor. He is very concerned about the counterfeit drugs."

In a groggy voice, I heard myself say, "Hola, Miguel, don't leave."

Chapter 13

The Plan

When I woke, it was dusk. Clean, fresh air blew in the small window, and I felt almost normal, except for my face and rib cage. My small room was crowded with people: Rat, Maria, Miguel, Ricki, Hugo, and my two friends Syl and Nancy. These were people I recognized and knew.

There were other people I didn't know: three other boys about Rat's age, two muscular big men, and two beautiful girls, about thirty. I had never seen any of them before. There weren't enough chairs to go around and several, including Rat and Maria, sat on my bed.

"Maria, who are these people, and why are they here staring at me in bed?"

"Sue, the boys are here to help Rat, their friend. The other people work in the medical profession in free clinics, and when they heard about what was going on and what happened to you from Miguel, they came begging to help. I thought, the more people to help the better. Hugo and I convinced them we cannot go to the police, as we don't know which of them to trust. They all agree. Rat called Hugo, and he called your two friends, who came right away. Whatever we plan on doing about this has to be done between us—and soon. We must talk and come up with a plan."

"Well, they say two heads are better than one, so surely the fifteen of us can come up with something."

"We think we came up with a plan while you were sleeping. Miguel will stay with you and me." Maria was a smart woman, and I knew her plan would be worth listening to.

"Look, you said the tattoo you saw on Señor Pablo's hand is really a stamp from a disco. He would only go to a high-class place! Sonya and Patti will go to the Hard Rock and look for him there." I figured Sonya and Patti were the two beautiful young women.

"Rat and his friends will stake out the parking lots. Nancy and Syl will go to the other big disco. We all have phones; make sure they are on. If anyone sees anything, phone us so we can meet."

"What about me, Maria? I want to be part of this!"

"Baby girl, I don't think your face would be accepted in those places. You still look like hell. Even with my good medical care, it hasn't been long enough for you to be seen in public." Maria showered a look of pity on me.

Jeez, if I looked as bad as that sympathetic look, I must even look worse than I thought.

"Toni and Chui are going to the port to watch for anything suspicious. Things usually are very quiet this time of night, so they will notice anything unusual. Any boat movement, especially if coming closer to shore, they will spot."

Rat suddenly stood and yelled, "The yacht had señora painted on her. I know her picture; she is painter, Frida, maybe. Hard to see in dark water."

"Oh, Rat, that is great! Now we can look for that boat also!" Maria gave him a crushing hug. "You are a sweetheart."

"Okay, let's get this show on the road; we only have a few hours. When we have someone—Señor Pablo Diaz, Captain Chun Lee, Silver Hair, or his thugs—we will bring them back here. Susan deserves to be in on the questioning and, with a hoodie on and my help, maybe can manage to go to the port and see the drugs dumped if we can find them. If we lean on someone hard enough, one is bound to crack. After what they did to Susan, believe me, I have no qualms about using a little force." Sweet, long-eyelashed Miguel had a furious look as he spoke.

He leaned in close to me and brushed my hair from my face. It was as gentle as his kiss had been. I wanted there to be many kisses and gentle touches. At least if I had any say in the matter, there would be. I put my hand on his face and received a wink! Awww, maybe he felt the same. That wink was something.

After everyone had departed, I thought I would never sleep with the anxiety and excitement. I hoped I hadn't sent these marvellous friends into danger because I knew what Silver Hair and his thugs were capable of firsthand. Maria is a tricky woman, and even with the loud Ranchero music blaring in the plaza, I soon drifted off. She must have put another of her magical powders in my drink. I wasn't sure if it was the crashing waves or Miguel's cell phone ringing that finally woke me.

"Miguel, who is it? Have they seen any of them yet? Has the boat moved?"

"Shush, Maria, the connection is bad, and I can't hear well."

Maria had her ear pressed to the side of Miguel's head, trying to hear also.

From his slight smile and narrowing eyes, I knew the news was good and surprising.

"Well, you'll never guess who is on the way here, accompanied by twelve men, boys, and girls, all waving guns!"

"Who?" Maria and I asked in unison.

"None other than Capitan Chun Lee, and from the sound of things, he's about ready to shit his pants. I think our little troop of soldiers has him quivering for his life."

"Wow, Chun Lee! That is great! His only job was to get the boat to port. I doubt he even is involved in the counterfeit drugs. He'll be frightened of losing his boat and getting sent to jail! We should be able to get him to do anything we want if we threaten him with that!" Maria nearly shouted.

I was so excited. My face had started to hurt again from talking and smiling so much.

"*Tranquilo*, Susan; everything will work out. If anyone has to kick him, I promise you can have the honour." Miguel laughed at me, but I knew he was dead serious about the counterfeit drugs and would do anything to stop them from coming to shore.

Silently the door opened, and everyone trooped in. My first thought was, where in hell did all the guns come from, but I kept my mouth shut. Even Syl and Nancy were waving them around like two lunatics. I'm positive it was the first time either had ever held one, and if it had gone off, they likely would have fainted dead away.

Chun Lee was tied at the hands and knees, supported by Toni and Chui. He stared straight at me with my bruised face, and I saw fear in his eyes. He knew. Rat passed me the knife, and I wobbly stood and took a step toward him. Chun backed up a step, but Toni and Chui forced him closer.

I don't think I have ever consciously hurt another living thing, but in that one moment, I wanted to hit and hit and hit him. I wanted his face to hurt as mine did, and I wanted to see blood drip from his lips. He saw it in my eyes before I came to my senses and realized he had not been on the yacht. He would have been with his boat, protecting his killer cargo.

I felt a hand cover mine and lower the knife to the gun tape around his knees. Miguel and I cut through the tape, pushing him to sit in the only vacant place in the room, my bed.

"Chun, we want to know where your boat is, and we want to know now. Do you understand? If you don't tell us, we will beat you to a pulp as they did Susan or, if you'd rather, turn you over to Señor Pablo Diaz. The choice is yours, but you only have a minute to decide your fate. You know certain death awaits you at the hand of Señor Diaz." Miguel certainly sounded tough and brutal.

For the first time, I found my voice and addressed Chun. "Chun, we will not hurt you. We only want to stop the bad drugs from coming into Mexico. They could kill thousands of people."

"Drugs? What drugs? I know nothing of drugs. I bring stolen treasures to Señor Diaz. He pay me well. We have to be secret because the governments no like it when national treasures are in hands of collectors. My shrimp boat is the perfect place to smuggle them close to shore."

Maria stepped in very close to Chun Lee. As she looked straight and deeply into his eyes, sadness filled hers. "Chun Lee, do you remember three or four years ago when many of your people had to get flu shots, and over two thousand died because the shots were bad?"

"Yes, my grandmother died, as did many cousins." Tears came to Chun's eyes, and I knew Maria had him.

"These are the same kind of bad drugs you have on your boat. Señor Diaz lies to you. They are not stolen treasures. If you care about saving lives, you will help us get rid of the bad drugs before they get into Mexico and then to another country and hurt or kill many people, maybe even more of your family."

Tears streamed down Chun Lee's face. "I didn't know. I know what I do is wrong, but my family needs the money, and the shrimp are not plentiful now in the bay. Yes, I will help you. My boat is tied to a buoy about a mile offshore. We can get on very easy. The cargo is wrapped in plastic and tied with rope. I have a marine winch running a rope up and over a tall outrigger at the stern on the ship's deck. This type of winch does not spool the rope around a spool; it simply pulls the rope and piles it up on the backside of the winch.

"The crew places the rope into a barrel to maintain order and prevent tangling as it exits. It also can lift and place heavy crates on the ship's deck as well. It can arrange these on the deck or in the hold of the ship. It is a good winch and easy to use. It will be nothing for us to lift out the crates and drop them overboard."

"Okay, Chun, let's talk. We need to figure out how we are going to do this." Miguel was taking control of the situation, and I knew he'd decide on the best plan to sink the drugs while keeping us safe.

"They say thirty hands are better than two, so I guess we fifteen should be in an okay position to get this handled. All of us together should be able to hoist the crates and dump them overboard. I just want to be rid of them and have my normal, boring life back." The urgency in my voice made it sound rough.

"Sue, I doubt you will ever have your normal, boring life back! I'll make sure of that later when we have finished with this horrible business! Now Chun, Hugo, and I need to talk about his boat. Please, Maria, get us pencils and paper. I need to learn all I can quickly about his shrimp boat and this winch. I think we need another plan. I don't think just the winch will work. Even together we are not strong enough to lift the cargo with it. Dumping it would not destroy it either, and we wouldn't have time anyway."

Miguel and Hugo huddled at the table with Captain Lee. Soon, the paper was covered with drawings of drafts, booms, and many other things that meant nothing to the rest of us, and we sort of ignored the talk except for Rat, Toni, and Chui. They were paying very close attention. Maria called me aside, and we sat on the bed while the men talked about the best plan.

"Susan, I have come to think a great deal of you. I wouldn't want you to get hurt. I saw just now the way Miguel looked at you. Be careful of him."

"Why would you warn me about your own brother, Maria? He has been wonderful. I like him very much."

Maria looked off into the distance and replied, "Susan, Miguel has a terrible reputation with women. Ever since his wife died giving birth to his dead son, he has gone from one affair to another with no feelings for the women he uses. Just be careful, and don't get hurt. He is charming and can talk his way into your life, only to drop you when he's finished with you. Watch him, stay friends, but don't fall for his sweet talk."

"Oh, Maria, we like each other, and this business with the drugs has made us conspirators. I'm sure there is nothing more. I appreciate your warning and will certainly take care of myself."

Even if I don't want to, I thought. Jeez, Miguel is everything a woman could want. I guess that's what makes it so easy for him to have any girl he wants. Well, this girl would heed the warning.

Maria patted my hand, and we switched our attention back to the men's conversation.

Captain Lee knew his boat well. Technically, the boat belonged to Señor Diaz, and Miguel found out it was heavily insured. With that knowledge, he ascertained that destroying it would be the better way of getting it out of commission forever. He also thought that even with fifteen of us, we would not have time to hoist all the crates to dump. He was too much of a gentleman to say because six of us were female, only insinuating that was one of the reasons.

The crates were constructed of slabs of wood and filled with a straw-like material for packing. The boat was forty-eight feet, built of cypress and juniper, with only a small pilothouse near the bow. Everything was on one level, leaving the hull for the engine, tanks, and room to work.

Miguel said the four stored tanks of propane Chun had told him about, plus the one connected to the water heater and stove, would be sufficient for blowing the boat to splinters the size of toothpicks! Chun Lee's eyes widened dramatically to silver-dollar size.

"Miguel, you can't blow up my boat! How will I make a living for my family? Señor Diaz will kill me if I destroy his boat."

"Chun, I've done a lot of research on this in the past couple of days. I know when the Feds, WHO, and IMPACT learn of our accomplishment tonight in keeping these drugs from being distributed in Mexico and exported to other countries, the reward will buy you a new boat of your own—one you will not have to do illegal work with or obey Señor Diaz."

"Oh yes, Miguel, that would be the kind of life I have only been able to dream of having! Let's go blow it to hell! I know how. One spark from anything down there, bilge pump or electrical wiring, and kaboom! Propane is heavier than air; leaks can cause it to collect and settle in low, enclosed areas. The smallest of sparks will cause this gas to ignite, and she'll sink within minutes, taking everything with her, except for the smallest pieces of wood that will float! All we have to do is empty the tanks." Captain Lee's excitement was contagious, and we were all wide-eyed and overloaded with adrenalin.

"That sounds like the plan, Chun. Now how do we go about this without blowing ourselves up as well?" Miguel always the answerable one for our safety.

"I'll run the boat out in darkness a few miles. You, Hugo, Toni, and Chui will follow in the dinghy. The rest of you will stay far enough away to see the explosion and be close enough to pick up any of us who happen to end up in the water. I don't see this happening, as we should be able to turn all five valves counterclockwise at the same time. Once the valves are open, the boat will flood with the propane. Let's synchronize our watches so we can be sure we open them at exactly the time we decide once we are on board. Then we can jump ship before a spark or something blows her. Remember, turn counterclockwise."

"Chun, you are a genius. Without you, we would be wandering around like an accident looking for a place to happen." Miguel was very pleased with Chun's plan and said he felt it was decent and good, as it would keep the rest of us safe.

Like cat burglars in dark clothing, my flaming red hair wrapped in a hoodie, we trooped down to the port with guns shoved in belts and pockets. It's amazing how much more confident you feel with a gun, and I was thankful my husband had taken time to teach me to shoot. I was good at it, too. Although I had never shot a human, I had shot bull's-eyes and small animals. Line the bottles in a row, and I'd take every one out. I considered these men to be killer animals.

Chun left first in the smallest dinghy to give him time to move the shrimper out. The rest of us talked over the plan for a few minutes, and then Hugo, Miguel, Toni, and Chui left in the second dinghy. They would meet the shrimper and help Chun turn on the propane valves. Rat and his three friends were to go on the banana boat, while Syl, Nancy, Sonya, and Patti went in their fishing panga with Ricki.

I was to stay on shore as a lookout with Maria but at the last minute couldn't stand it and jumped on the banana boat as Rat was pushing off. Picking up a paddle, I started paddling and fought back tears from the pain in my side, but no way in hell was I getting left behind, broken rib or not.

"Sue, what you do?" Rat was angry and screaming at me to get off.

"Rat, I can't stay behind. All my friends are out here, and I'm going to be too. So just paddle. We need to stay beside each other, as Miguel said, but separated to cover more area."

"Okeydoke, Sue. You tell Miguel it your idea not mine. Maria and Miguel very mad at you and me. Miguel said you to stay with Maria. Miguel always knows better thing to do. He say Maria need talk with you about special plan."

I could hear Maria screaming my name and yelling to come back. I wished she'd be quiet, as Miguel had said to.

"Rat, I promise to explain everything to them. You will not be blamed. Now for heaven's sake, just be quiet and paddle. Maria is making enough noise for all of us."

Chapter 14

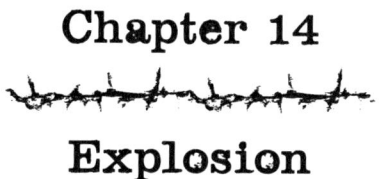

Explosion

We paddled in the pitch black for more than an hour. It was slower going without the motors, but we didn't dare use them. We could hear the oars and paddles dipping in and out of the water from the others, but there was no sound of human voices.

Ahead, a small point of light blinked three times, and we knew this was Miguel's signal for us to stop and wait. I counted to three hundred, trying to keep track of five minutes. After three times I gave up. Fifteen minutes had passed if I had counted correctly.

What could possibly be taking them so long? Enough time had passed for them to have opened the valves. I wondered how long the propane would take to fill the hull. No one had talked about that, and how did we know a spark would occur to set it off? More important, no one had said how long they would be on board or what would happen should a spark occur before they managed to get off. I guess that outcome was unspeakable.

Bang! A small gunshot rang out over the water. We were all holding our breath, waiting for another, when the water exploded into the night sky, lighting it brighter than fireworks or the New York City lights! Then came the blast and noise. A boom so loud we covered our ears, and the boats rocked in the waves caused by the detonation.

Oh God, it had happened! The gunshot had been the spark. But where were the men? Even in the bright firelight left on the horizon, I could not make out shapes of boats coming toward us. Everyone was paddling toward the explosion as fast as they could get paddles in and out of the water. Small pieces of debris, burning and burnt wood, and sparks showered down on us. Larger pieces were floating by, none large enough to hold a man.

The fire wavered and dropped into the ocean, hissing and spitting like a dragon dying. We knew the shrimper was gone and prayed that it and its cursed load had gone to the ocean floor, never to be seen again.

I could hear a hissing sound and saw Rat holding his hands over a piece of hot wood that had punctured the rubber banana. Water poured into the hollow air space, and the banana started sinking like a pricked balloon. Front and back lifted from the water as the middle went into the sea. As I had been last on, I was first to be thrown up and off as the rear end of the banana lifted. The sudden motion somersaulted me headfirst into the dark water.

"Miguel, Rat," I screamed automatically as I felt my body, wet and heavy, slowly swallowed by the water.

Chapter 15

Pickup

The black, pitch-black, foul-tasting, salty ocean was not to be the death of me. I kicked and struggled to orient myself, trying to find the direction to the surface. The current was pulling at me, and I knew the tide was coming in, so I would be closer to shore than when I went under. I burst to the surface, gasping and sputtering for a mouthful of air.

"Rat, Rat." I tried to scream his name over the sound of the waves. I floated on top and in and out of the waves, trying to keep the pieces of debris away from me. I swam for what I knew to be the shoreline and, when out of breath, floated on my back. Everything was cold, dark, and empty. I felt like I was the only person left on earth. I was on my back when I heard something other than waves. What was it?

A whirling sound? What was whirling? A bright pinpoint of light was shining down on me, and the whirling was coming from the light. It was a helicopter. Someone, likely the police, was here to see what the explosion had been. I'd be happier if it were the news channel crew, not knowing which police to trust. My luck was telling me this likely wouldn't be the case.

A lifesaver was dropped near me, and kicking off my runners, I swam for it. Whoever it was, it had to be better than drowning.

As I was being hoisted up, I searched the water surface in their lights trying to see Rat or his friends. Since we had all dressed in dark clothing, there was no bright spot of colour to see. The wind from the helicopter blades was making the water choppier than just the wave action. It was impossible to see anything. Swaying with the force of the blade wind, I finally got up to the opening in the side of the chopper. A hand reached for me and dragged me over the edge. I looked up into the face of the man who had saved me.

Okay, so what was I, a magnet for trouble? I was looking into the face of the fat bald man with the Italian accent, certain this was the man Rat had described.

I screamed, "No," trying to pull back. I wanted to get away from him and would have jumped back into the ocean had he not held me tightly, wrapping me in a warm blanket.

"Miss Shaw, please calm down. I am an IMPACT officer. I'm here to stop the importing of the counterfeit drug shipment, and I needed the photo of Pablo Diaz to try to find him. That was why I searched your apartment and looked in your bag. I was not involved with the car that tried to run you down. That was Edwin Louis Romano, an agent let go from IMPACT for his conduct, the man you call Silver Hair. He stole my ID and changed the photo to his. My name is Stefano Orlando Sorrentino. I've been watching you and him to see who found the photo and of what significance it was to each of you."

Oh, my heavens, how much more complicated could this get? I knew this man was telling the truth.

"Where are the others? Rat, his three friends, and I were on the banana boat when a piece of burning wood hit it, and I was thrown into the ocean! Where are the others? Are you searching the waters?"

"Slow down, Miss Shaw. All are safe on shore except for Captain Chun Lee and Rat. We expect the current has moved them away from our search area but expect to find them soon. The shore patrol is almost here, and the other helicopter is still looking. During the search, there were no bodies spotted. We are sure we will find them." He ordered the pilot to land.

"Now I must get you to shore so Doctora Maria can treat you. Doctor Miguel will be most pleased to see you alive. He has been going up and down the beach shouting your name since he has been ashore."

Landing on the beach caused a windstorm of blasting sand that didn't stop Miguel from ducking down and running to the copter door. Arms reached in and lifted me out.

"Oh, Susan, are you hurt? I was afraid I had lost you!"

Tucked in Miguel's arms, I wanted to spend the rest of my life there.

"No, Miguel, I'm fine. Just wet and cold, and I could use a breath of fresh air. We have no time for anything now except to help find Chun and Rat. They have to be all right, they have to be. Rat has become a son to me. I can't lose him now. I love him."

I was still out of breath but had to know what had happened while I had been taking my scary swim. "Have you heard any news at all? Did the IMPACT agent, Señor Sorrentino, explain everything to you? Can we trust the police that came with him? Oh, Miguel, tell me everything. What are we to do?"

I hadn't noticed Maria joining us, replacing the wet blanket with a lovely, warm, and dry one. Miguel slowly was leading us away from the activity.

"So many people are here! Who are they all? I don't see the girls or the boys."

"They have been taken to our clinics or your place. Sonya and Patti are taking care of them and outfitting them with dry clothing. There were no serious injuries, just scrapes and a few bruises from the flying debris," Maria answered. "Some of the people are residents attracted by the blast; others are news crews. The rest are police and shore patrol. Every fisherman and boat owner is here to help in the search for Rat and Chun."

Miguel had us now at a distance from everyone else. He wrapped me in his arms and whispered in my ear. "Susan, do not show any reaction to what I say to you. Maintain your normal behaviour to this situation and show your emotions at losing Rat and Chun. Do you understand?"

I nodded yes into his shoulder although not knowing what he was talking about. He loosened his hold on me but kept me close to his face.

In the moonlight, with police whirling red and blue lights, it would appear only that Miguel was filling me in on the news that Rat and Chun had not been found. Maria stood close by, separating herself to give us more privacy.

Miguel put his hands on either side of my face so we were eye to eye.

"Susan, Rat and Chun are both safe." His hands tightened on my head to hold me still and quiet as I squirmed.

"What do you mean, safe? If this is true, why are you still searching for them?"

"It was a part of Sorrentino's plan. No one but Chun, Rat, Maria, and I knew. I'm sorry, Susan, you would have known if you had stayed on shore because Maria would have clued you in. Your fiery personality took off, and you jumped on the banana. She didn't get a chance to talk to you."

"Yes, I can't hold anyone responsible for that except myself. Miguel, where are they, and why are they being hidden?"

"We want Señor Pablo Diaz to think they are dead. When he discovers the shipment and his boat have been destroyed, he will hold Chun liable and likely try to kill him. We must have Pablo and his henchmen in custody before Chun is discovered washed ashore alive, understand?"

"Yes, I get it, and it is a great idea. If Pablo is in jail for the rest of his life, Chun can truly have a good life. Will the reward for destroying the drugs go to him?" I could see good things coming from this.

"I believe the reward will and the insurance also. Pablo wanted no ties to the drug trade so had listed Chun as beneficiary for the boat insurance. He will have enough to obtain a good shrimper and move with his family to a new location."

"Oh, Miguel, you are an angel and smart as hell to have figured a way out of this for all of us." I smiled into his eyes. Then remembering Maria's warning, I stepped away from him and reached for her hand.

"Well, without the cooperation of Señor Sorrentino, it would not have been possible. He has been after Diaz for years and will do most anything to end this. There is one condition, though, that you may not agree with. If we are needed again to help in a case of other counterfeit drugs entering our country we are to help him in return. How do you feel about that?"

"Miguel, I have never felt so alive, important, strong, and helpful in my life." I held Maria's hand and drew her closer until the three of us were in a circle of clasped hands. "We will fight the good fight. We will do what we can. My two dear doctors, we shall be the three musketeers, all for one, and one for all!"

With that cry, we three raised our hands in the air, a bond as strong as blood brothers would have.

I happened to glance in the direction of Sorrentino and saw the smile on his face. He understood what had just happened and very likely understood more than we thought he did.

Chapter 16

Free of the Bad Guys

We started walking toward the group of onlookers, agents, and media people. I certainly didn't want anything to do with the media and hoped Sorrentino and his agents were taking care of that. Suddenly, a police car came roaring up the beach to an abrupt stop, spitting sand in every direction. The urgency in the air was potent. Sorrentino spoke with the officer, and for a big man, he managed a jump in the air of about three feet with a bellow of victory.

"We got him! We got him; we got Diaz. He was surrounded at his home and, after a ten-minute shootout, was hit several times and now lies dead on his doorstep! He thought we were there to arrest him for a murder he had taken part in a couple of years ago and came out shooting. Chun Lee is safe, and the biggest importer of counterfeit pharmaceuticals in Mexico is gone! His henchmen are all in custody, giving up as soon as they saw him dead."

A cheer went up from all. Then, suddenly, everyone was quiet. The search for Chun Lee and Rat was to continue.

Miguel could not share the knowledge of their safety just yet. There would be many days of paperwork and talking to the police and agencies, and of the reward and insurance. We had to be absolutely sure both would go to Chun Lee. We didn't know exactly where they had escaped to, but his wife and children were not at the house, so we guessed he had made a good choice of a hiding place. I felt certain Rat was safe with them. He would know how to contact us.

Maria returned to her clinic, saying she could do nothing to help with the search and the people at the clinic needed her attention. Miguel and I walked to my apartment, where I was almost kissed to death by Princess as soon as she saw me. I didn't mind the pain in my ribs while holding her close. I was so glad to see her healthy and happy. I was grateful she recognized me with my face still swollen many shades of blue, green, and yellow.

Miguel waited patiently while I took a long hot shower before we returned to the clinic. His impatience showed as I walked out, wrapped only in a towel, to find a clean outfit. He jumped from the chair, whipped me around to face him, and with a grouchy voice told me to put on my clothes and stop parading in front of him. I could see his desire for me in his eyes and through his well-fitted jeans. His words were lies to his body's reaction. He was dead tired, and it showed on his face, but he lowered his hands and tightened the towel around my body.

"Susan, sweet Sue, I wish we had met many years ago. Things might have been different for us. It's too late now. Go put clothes on, and stay away from me. I have nothing to offer you."

"Miguel, I lost my husband. I understand we never could or would want to replace them. We can have each other, enjoy each other. That is enough for me. Could it be enough for you? Could you forget about your other distractions?"

Laughing and nodding his head yes, he stripped naked. I have to admit he did have help in that department. Then, taking my hand, he led me back into the shower and under a stream of hot water ran his hands over my body and entered me slowly. The sound of my beating heart was lost, mingling with the running water.

We soaped each other slowly with tender touches. His mouth closed around one nipple, and my whole body shook with desire. He drew it into his mouth while making moaning sounds—maybe that was me, hard to tell. His lips moved over mine, and his tongue slipped into my mouth. The water had turned from hot to cool by the time he lifted me in his arms and walked to the bedroom. I hadn't realized how far it was from the shower to my bed, and I wanted to yell run. Maybe I did because, at that instant, he lowered me to the bed and lay beside me.

"Susan, my sweet, maybe I was wrong. Maybe we do belong to each other. Will we continue as lovers? Or will we stay companions and part of the three musketeers?"

I saw from the smile in his eyes and on his lips he knew damn well he didn't need to ask. "Yes, Miguel, I want to make love to you forever. Please, please, now, I need you again now."

He entered me softly, gently, filling my complete body with him.

"Your face and ribs, my sweet Sue, are still so bruised and sore. I want you desperately but don't want to cause you more pain."

"Oh, for God's sake, Miguel, stop thinking and shut up. Just make love to me. I can't stand it any longer; I need you so. Love me, Miguel, just love me as you want and need to. I want and need the same thing."

I felt as if it was my first time with a man. I felt everything, not just in my body but in my heart, mind, and soul. Tears were on both our faces as we climaxed the last time together.

We knew each of us had found love again. There would be no replacing our first loves. The past was the past. We could see this was a new beginning for each of us. We had found new love. Jeez, at my age, I had just discovered I could have true love again.

Hours later, after much talking about our lives and sharing of secrets, I knew I had been right to ignore Maria's warning. Miguel had been searching to fill his heart again. I gave thanks that he had found it with me. We showered and walked to his clinic, although we both needed sleep.

Chapter 17

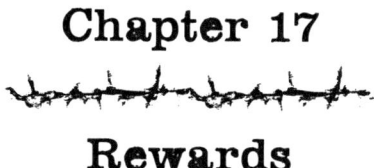

Rewards

A month after speaking with several lawyers for IMPACT and the insurance investigator, Miguel determined it was safe for Chun Lee to return and claim his reward and insurance money. Señor Pablo Diaz was dead. There had been no problem getting his henchmen jailed. It would be years before they even got to trial, and there was no danger of them getting off with anything less than life sentences. Deported to Italy, Edwin Louis Romano, the darn traitor, would be a guest of its prison for many years.

Early the next morning, Miguel arrived at our house to pick me up for the trip north to tell Chun and his family. Yes, you heard me correctly, our house. We couldn't stand being separated even for one night, and Miguel had moved me into a lovely seaside villa with a pool and lavish gardens. I felt like a kept woman, but that was fine. I knew Miguel had come to love me. Maria was pleased with our arrangement and understood from Miguel's changed attitude that he was committed.

I had explained to Maria that if it only was to be for a short time, I didn't care and would deal with the outcome later. Right now I wanted to share Miguel's life and love as long as I could. I couldn't let this wonderful man out of my life completely.

Maria had smiled a sly smile and told me this was the first time Miguel had taken a woman into his home. It was a dream house and, when I complained about the price, was given a huge surprise. Maria informed me their grandfather had been an extremely successful ranchero, and they had inherited everything. It was still a working business and doing well with the exportation of bananas, mangoes, coconuts, tobacco, and avocados to Canada, the United States, and South America.

The free clinics existed because a share of the profits was donated by the plantation administration to maintain them. This kind and thoughtful brother and sister gave me another reason to love them. Their generosity was unlimited to their employees and their town.

After Miguel picked me up and drove several hours, we came to a small house that Chun had found as refuge for his family. It was a lovely white cottage outside of town on a cliff. His wife, Medang, could stand on the high cliff bank and watch for the boats coming back to the dock for the day with their catch. She had a garden planted, and pots of herbs sat on each of the windowsills. Flowering shrubs lined the brick walkway to the door, which stood open to let in the ocean breezes and sunlight. Glass sparkled in each of the large windows.

"Miguel, this looks like a fairy cottage! It's so peaceful and beautiful!"

"I agree, sweetheart. Chun and Medang have a charming home and want to make it their permanent home. They have no interest in relocating."

Chun, Medang, and their children came running down the walk to throw their arms around us in greeting.

"Susan, Miguel, we are so pleased to see you and thought the hour would never come when you were to arrive. Please, enter our humble abode. Medang has tea prepared for you after your long journey."

"With great pleasure, Chun, we will take tea with you. Thank you."

We removed our sandals at the door and entered into a beautiful room, a mixture of Mexican and Chinese that blended perfectly to give off a calming, peaceful aura.

"Please feel free to break custom and discuss business over tea. We are most anxious to hear the latest news from you in person and not just what we get over the Internet."

I giggled! I could not help it. The thought of these graceful people—such a tiny little woman—in this fairy cottage using the Internet was beyond my imagination.

"Sorry, the tea tickled my throat!"

The wink Miguel sent me said he understood how I felt. We were so attuned to each other by now that he seemed to read my thoughts, sometimes knowing what I was thinking or going to say before I did. How I loved this man who was also my best friend!

Chun was overcome by the amount of the reward, which was a percentage of the drugs' worth. When told the insurance Señor Diaz had on the shrimper was over two million pesos, I thought he would have a heart attack. Glad Miguel was a doctor.

"Oh, Miguel, I could not accept this large amount of money. It should be split among all who helped. I did very little." Tears were in his eyes, and he reached to hold his wife's hand.

"Yes, Chun, I agree. Without everyone, we could not have pulled this off, but without you, there would have been no way for us to accomplish it. The money is yours. You can enlarge your home with more bedrooms, send your children to college, and maybe visit your families in China before you start working on your very own shrimper that you will no doubt be buying. You can do as you like with the money. It's yours."

Tears filled the eyes of both Chun and his wife, but before anything else could be said, I was grabbed from behind so powerfully that I fell from my knees at the tea table. Rat kept his arms around me, hugging and saying, "Sue, Sue, my Sue, you came for me!"

"Rat," I cried, clasping him in a bear hug, "Oh, my darling boy, how I have missed you."

Chun and Medang laughed and explained that they had kept our coming as a surprise for Rat because he had been such a help to them; they wanted to give him something special. He would be sharing any money used for their children's education, as one of their own.

Miguel intervened, saying Francisco was to be part of our family now and our son.

Rat and Medang joined hands and danced around the room. Medang sang, "A wedding to plan, a wedding to plan, how wonderful. What fun."

"Well, Medang, nothing has been said about a wedding. We are trying to see if we fit together, and right now we are living in the same house. Maybe someday we can speak of marriage."

Miguel dashed Medang's happiness and mine but soon restored it.

"First we will plan a fiesta for the whole town, all our families and friends, while they are here to celebrate the destruction of the drugs and the happiness for you. Chun, you and your family will stay at our ranch, as will Sue's friends. We will all be together for a great party, music, and dance. It will be an outstanding celebration to be shared by all."

A gigantic fiesta? This was news to me. And a house large enough for dozens of guests? I was overwhelmed.

"Susan will be my mother! God hears my prayers and answers. I'm to be a son! I no more live in the dump. I live with Susan and Princess now. I no longer Rat; I am Francisco. I will be a good son."

Rat, no, Francisco was dancing and crying, singing and yelling at the same time. Miguel and I held our arms out, and Francisco fell into them. I hoped that this would be permanent. Miguel still had never mentioned marriage. He seemed quite content to have me as a kept woman. It was fine with me. I didn't care as long as we were together, but I prayed that for Francisco his newfound happiness and life would be a forever thing.

When the excitement settled, Miguel took Chun aside, and they put their John Henrys on the many sheets of necessary papers to finalize the payout of insurance and reward monies to Chun. Chun asked for advice, and Miguel said he would arrange all the proper documents with his lawyers and accountant. The bank would accept the deposits and, with the accountant's help, disperse them, as Chun desired, with trust funds for all the children. The labourers from the ranch would help with the extension of Chun's cottage.

Everything seemed almost too perfect. I felt uneasy in the pit of my stomach. What was wrong with me? Goose bumps ran up and down my arms. I shivered in the heat.

"Come, Susan, it is time for us to go home. Francisco will stay here, as his school term ends next week, and return to us for good when they all come for the fiesta the following week."

With that said, Miguel led me to the car and closed the door. I turned to stare out the back windshield and saw Francisco, Chun, Medang, and the children waving and calling good-byes frantically as the car gained speed and turned the curve to head down the twisted hillside road. My goose bumps were back, and I shivered again.

Chapter 18

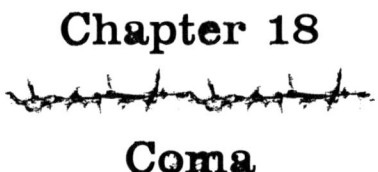

Coma

"My soul, Miguel, what the hell are you doing? Slow down!" I glanced over at him and saw astonishment on his face. His foot was pumping up and down, keeping time to a beat of some kind of crazy music, and he yelled, "Sue, there's no brakes!" As he was saying this, the car accelerated, swerving around a curve to the left, barely staying upright on two wheels. Before the car had a chance to bang down on all fours, a steep curve to the right picked it up, and this time there weren't two wheels left on the road.

"Hang on, head down!" Miguel was screaming at me, but I couldn't take my eyes off the sky in front of us with the clouds rising over us. Then I realized the clouds weren't rising; we were falling. It felt like flying.

"Sue, brace yourself!"

The bottom of the car hit the tops of some trees and flipped over. I was upside down and then sitting up and I wished the damn woman screaming would stop. It was hurting my head. The car landed with a sudden stop. The screaming had also stopped. Everything was quiet and peaceful, so I floated on the surface of the quiet.

I drifted along on white foggy stuff that surrounded me. I was warm and soft, completely comfortable.

"Oh Lord, please hear our prayers." Maria's voice was in the fog too.

I floated farther looking for her, but no matter where I stretched my arms, I could not find her.

"Doctor, when will she wake up?" Syl was speaking now.

I floated, now looking for Syl. I could hear her but couldn't see her. What did she mean, wake up? I wasn't sleeping.

My daughter was in the fog! How did she get here?

"Damn you, Susan, open your eyes! Come back to me, please" I could hear Miguel's tears in his cry to me. "Oh God, I love you so! I can't live without you now. Come back to me. I can't lose you, my love."

Was he speaking to me? I struggled to open my eyes and groaned with the pain in my head.

"She's waking up! She's coming out of the coma!" Several people were talking at the same time.

I looked up into the face I loved, tears glistening on his cheeks, and tried to speak but couldn't. A soft touch on the lips and then drops of cool water moistened my mouth.

Again I tried to speak and this time managed one word: "What?"

"Susan, we had a car accident when we left Chun's house. You have been in a coma for two days. You have no other injuries except for the hit on the head. Your daughter, son, and all your family are here. I must get Cassy from the lunchroom. They have been tormented with worry."

"You?"

"I have a cut on one arm. See my bandage with all the tape? Now rest a few minutes while I get the doctor and Cassy. She will want to talk. I have explained everything to them, so don't waste your strength by trying to fill her in."

I closed my eyes and this time was not floating in any white fog.

Another splitting head! It seemed most of my time in Mexico was filled with head injuries and pain. I was beginning to feel like a fly waiting for a hit with a swatter.

No, there were friends; Francisco, my soon-to-be new son; and Miguel, my love and friend. Any pain I endured was nothing compared to my gain. No pain, no gain. I've said that many times.

Cassy, my emotional daughter, ran into the room, "Mum, Mum, oh Mum! How do you get into these messes? Just look at you."

"Cassy, shush, I have a headache. Miguel explained everything to you. You know what and why things happened. I know the girls have been talking your ear off. Everything is fine, and everything is going to get better."

"Yes, Mum, I do understand. I was just afraid I'd lose you. I know about the fiesta and wedding. Miguel has invited us to stay at his ranch until after the wedding. We are so pleased you will be honeymooning in Canada. The kids will be so happy to see you and meet Miguel."

"Honeymoon in Canada? Wedding? What wedding? What are you talking about? Miguel and I have not talked about getting married. It's never been mentioned."

"Mum, all Miguel has talked about since we got here is having you as his wife, about marrying his love. Wondering how he'd live without you. Of course, there is a wedding."

"Well, I guess you know more than me. The planning continued evidently while I was knocked out. Miguel has not asked me to get married."

"Mum, everyone is so wonderful, and they are all so happy for you and love you. Sometimes you're dumber than dumber. Reminds me of the time you cut your hair and dyed it. You're always doing dumb things. Now is not the time to be stupid. Of course you'll say yes when he asks you. You sure turned out to be something. I must run; we are all meeting for dinner and then going to the ranch! I'm so tired after the plane trip and sitting with you, but I'm way too excited for sleep yet."

"Whoa, everyone? That means I am going to be here alone? How can my family and friends treat me so cruelly?" I laughed.

"Miguel and Maria thought it best for you to have a quiet night and good sleep while twenty or thirty people get settled in. That way you will miss all the confusion. Miguel says you can come tomorrow."

"Really? Ahh, I understand. If I'm a good girl and do as I'm told, I can be treated tomorrow. He's giving the orders already, is he? Okay, I think it's a good plan. I want to go to the ranch tomorrow to be with everyone. If I have to behave myself for one night, I guess it's okay. I am so tired anyway, and an uneventful night's sleep is likely what I need. You know, Cassy, I haven't been to the ranch yet. I am very excited to see it; the description sounds unbelievable. Good night, sweetie. I love you, and for heaven's sake, get some sleep too."

"See you in the morning, Mum. I'm so glad you're awake. The specialist assured us after his examination you are fine now that you are awake and out of the coma. I was so worried, but now I just feel so excited, and I know you are okay. Sleep well. I love you."

I wanted to say "you too," but didn't get a chance, as I fell asleep before I could open my mouth.

Chapter 19

Meeting the Ranch

Turning off the road, we went down a lovely interlocking gray brick roadway. Trees and flowers of every colour God had come up with lined the lawn beside the bricks. I could see why they called it El Rancho de Floras.

Suddenly in front of us was a long, white building that formed a courtyard with a cistern. The water, from a five-foot-high cement hyacinth, flowed over the stone artwork. The middle of the building was a story taller than the two wings.

Miguel explained that both wings contained bedrooms, each with a bath. The centre contained the great room, while the kitchen and dining room were to the sides. During the rule of Diaz, it had received a facelift in the form of a proud neoclassical style.

On the left, toward the back, I could see an old sugar mill and an area dedicated to the growing of organic earthworms for composting, also an important industry, I learned. To the right was an old chapel restored with a steeple pointing to the deep blue sky.

The many flowers, sugarcane, and earthy smell of fertile dirt filled my senses and my lungs with clean, natural sensations I had forgotten existed.

The white of the house shimmered in the sun, and the brass bell in the tower of the little chapel glistened a bright gold. What a wondrous sight! If I were asked and answered yes, this would be my home! I knew we couldn't live here full time, as Miguel's lovely beach home was closer to his work at the clinics. So this self-supporting ranch would be used as a vacation getaway home. It also would provide lodging for family and guests when they came.

Under the arches on the porch, which ran the full length of the building, were comfortable seating areas and tables of sleek dark wood, polished as highly as jewels. Large potted plants were placed perfectly to look like part of the house. I had difficulty speaking; the beauty had taken my breath away.

Suddenly, a yapping dog jumped into my arms, lavishing kisses all over my face.

"Oh, Miguel, thank you for bringing Prin. I was worried about her and missed her." Prin nestled in my arms, and I was content to let her stay there. "You should have prepared me for such a magnificent home. When you said ranch, I pictured a log building with bunk houses."

"Susan, the beauty of this ranch dims in my sight when I look at you and know you love me. Our love will make it shine even more."

Entering the huge double front doors carved with wild animals and birds, I stood looking at the most gorgeous room I could ever have imagined. An enormous chandelier with candle-shaped bulbs glistened above. The back wall was a floor-to-ceiling rock fireplace a man could walk in. My first thought was I'm happy to know there are people who clean because I sure as hell couldn't keep up this place.

As I admired the grandeur of the collectible artwork and antique figurines of leopards and lizards, Aztec figures, and pots, I realized there were people mingling everywhere: Francisco and his three friends, Ricki, Hugo, Chun, his wife Medang, their children, and Toni and Chui. Syl and Nancy were talking to Sonya and Patti. Maria stood with arms stretched out to me, a huge smile of genuine happiness on her face.

"Welcome, Sue. We are all so happy you have recovered, and now with your friends and family here, we can have the fiesta and dance!"

My daughter, her husband, my son, his wife, and my sister walked into the room. All threw their arms around me, almost knocking me over. Prin jumped to the floor to escape the onslaught.

"My heavens, what a great surprise! I knew Cassy was here, but Edward and May, what a bombshell to see you all here."

I threw my arms around my older sister, Joan. "Oh, Joan, I'm so glad you too are here. You've told me so many times you'd never travel to Mexico again, and here you are."

"Susie, you didn't think I'd stay home when my baby sister is in a coma? You know me better than that."

"You can thank Miguel for that! He refused to take no for an answer. We flew here right after the accident. Wow, what a change first class is from economy flights! That's the way to travel. Of course, it didn't take too much persuasion. We all wanted to be here as soon as we heard about your car accident and the unfortunate encounter with the drug dealer, and we wanted to meet Miguel and Maria, and see your new home. We knew you weren't one to stay in a coma and miss all this." My son, Edward, was beaming with joy. I can't remember when last I had seen him display that much emotion or talk so much at one time.

I hugged each of them close to me and whispered how much I loved them. Then Maria broke into the conversation to say dinner was served, and the twenty-three of us walked to the dining room, where the vast table was laid out in royal style.

Hand-painted antique glazed settings with silver flatware and crystal glasses sparkled under the candlelight. Several young women stood ready to serve, and the food was indescribable.

After dinner, we retired to the back of the room for a liqueur and delightful Mexican coffee in front of the fireplace. I thought everyone would be too full to even breathe let alone talk, but almost immediately, the discussion began about the party, music, dancers, and food.

"Hey, friends, slow down!" Miguel stood to move to the centre of the room. "I haven't asked Susan yet to marry me. I was waiting for a more private moment to ask, but the happiness, love, and friendship in this room right now make it the perfect spot. I just hope she'll say yes and not make me a fool in front of all of you."

Everyone moaned, "No, never could happen. Just look at her eyes and smile."

"Well, let's see." Miguel knelt in front of me and took my hand. "Susan O'Brien Shaw, will you be my wife and take me as your husband?"

Suddenly a massive diamond was coming toward my left hand.

"Yes, yes, I will, but I will never wear that ring! I'd be terrified every moment of losing it."

Miguel gathered me in his arms. "My dearest, the ring had to be beautiful enough to reflect the love in our hearts."

As the tears rolled down the girls' faces, I realized I also was crying.

Maria shouted, "Gracias Dios! I thought he'd never get around to asking. It's now official. Where do we start?"

Laughing, Miguel answered, "By asking Sue what kind of wedding she would like to have!"

"Small," I cried. "In the little chapel here on the ranch."

"But, Sue, there will be hundreds of guests. The chapel is too small." Maria was wringing her hands.

"Then we'll have two. One for us in the chapel and a short service on the lawn by the pool for other guests," I calmly answered. "The service in the chapel will only be for us here together."

Maria clapped her hands. "Perfect," she exclaimed. Then everyone was talking at once.

Not much got decided upon that evening, but it didn't matter. Everyone was laughing, drinking smooth tequila, and getting to know everything about each other and the ranch.

I knew in the following few days, Maria, Miguel, Cassy, and my sister and I, along with my two best friends, would work out the plans. Tonight was a night only to enjoy the love filling the room. A girl appeared and said she would show us to our rooms. I still could not believe this home was large enough to sleep so many people. I giggled. Cassy asked me what was so funny.

"Well, honey, if the crops fail, I can open a bed-and-breakfast!" I was giggling as my head hit the pillow, but it also could have been the tequila.

Chapter 20

Wedding Plans

The planning took off early the next morning. In a couple of hours, the mariachi, minister, piñatas, and food were booked and ordered. Extra staff was hired, and a big band for dancing was on its way.

"Miguel, there seems nothing for the girls and me to do! Everything is being done so quickly and easily! What can we do?"

"Well, my dear, nothing for the fiesta, but I suggest you get together and plan your dresses, flowers, and guest list for the chapel service. I think I heard Maria say she wanted to speak to you this morning concerning your dress. I believe she is in the *cocina*."

I found the kitchen and Maria. She ran toward me. "Susan, please come with me. I have something I want you to see."

We walked down the hallway and entered a huge bedroom filled with a seating area, walk-in closets, and a four-poster, queen-sized canopy bed with a stunning, carved wooden chest at the foot. There were hearts, angels, and the Lady of Guadalupe mingling beautifully with flowers and birds. The chest was very old and carved with love by hand.

"This will be your and Miguel's room. It was our parents' and is only used by the owner and his wife. We have not used it since our parent's death, but I had it redone for Miguel so it would be ready for him when he was. She walked to the chest, opened it, and unfolded the most beautiful wedding dress I had ever seen. Exquisite handmade lace hung from under the bustline to the floor. A diamond comb with a long veil hung beside it.

"Oh, Maria, this is so beautiful! It looks old Spanish and must be worth a fortune!"

"It was worn by my grandmother and mother. It would be an honour to our family if you consented to wear it as your wedding dress. I know it's not today's style, and if you'd rather have newer, please say so. We will understand."

"Oh, Maria, I would be honoured to wear it. You should be the one to carry on the family tradition. It is a gown of love and history, and I doubt it will fit me anyway. Look at the waist! Your mother must have had a waist about eighteen inches!" I said this as I glanced down at my twenty-six inches.

"Susan, I will not ever marry. I lost my fiancé in an accident. I was with him and also hurt and scarred. I cannot bear children and made the decision never to marry. Miguel is next in line, and you are the one he has chosen to wear this dress. His first wife was not asked to wear it as at that time it was still thought I would. Anna, please enter."

Maria's words brought an old, shrivelled lady into the room. Her back was bent, her hair long and white as the driven snow. She reached for the dress and touched it with soft movements of love. "Mistress, is it finally time? Am I to work with the miracle dress again?" she asked Maria in a voice so flowing and musical I could hardly distinguish the words.

"Yes, my friend, it is time."

"Susan, this is Anna. She is a seamstress and will fit the gown to your body. Believe me, she altered this dress for my grandmother and mother. There is extra material to alter it again for you. Anna knows this dress well, and the stitches will never be visible."

Anna and I nodded to each other, and her eyes seemed to smile at me. She had the look of a mysterious angel. Her eyes sparkled like her voice.

"Maria, why did she call it a miracle dress?"

"Susan, Anna believes this dress brings everlasting love to those who wear it. Each woman who has worn it had good fortune and the love of a soul mate for her entire life. Anna tatted the lace material to make the dress."

"Oh, my soul, Maria, how old is she? You said your grandmother wore it." I was amazed.

"Anna will soon be over a hundred years old. We really don't know her true age for sure. She was the first to wear it." Maria smiled at the lady standing in front of us still touching the lace with tiny old fingers, her eyes filled with love. "Anna was my grandmother's servant and great friend. She has lived at this ranch since being brought here from the mountains as an orphan when only a very small girl."

I blossomed at her words. I knew beyond a shadow of doubt the dress would be altered to fit me impeccably. A miracle dress to wear on a dream day!

Chapter 21

The Wedding

We planned to hold the wedding the day after the party. Cassy, Edward, and the rest of the family had to return to Canada for work. Miguel and Maria were anxious to get back to their clinics. Their friends and neighbours had work awaiting them also.

When I went outside, I could barely believe the changes that had been accomplished in such a short time. The area surrounding the pool held a floral-decorated arch, a newly constructed wooden dance floor, and piñatas hanging everywhere. Long banquet tables fanned out from the arch with all of the chairs facing it. The chairs were covered in smooth white linen. Tied to the back of each chair was a large ribbon bow, each containing a coloured flower.

I stood for several moments taking it all in because I knew when the time came to stand under the arch, I would see nothing but Miguel. I felt hands encircle my waist and turned into them.

"Is something not to your liking, my dear?" Miguel asked anxiously.

I laughed into his eyes. "Good heavens, no! Everything is perfect. Even more than I could have dreamed. How was so much accomplished without waking me?"

"Well, I told everyone double pay if it was completed during the night. I knew after tequila you and your family would sleep like babies!" Miguel laughed.

"You mean you poured strong drinks on purpose to put us to sleep?"

Still laughing, Miguel said, "No. I knew you were not used to tequila and would sleep soundly."

Suddenly the chill and goose bumps were running down my arms and across my neck.

"Goodness, Sue, are you cold?" he asked, a worried look on his face. "Are you feeling well? Maybe it is prewedding jitters. Everything has happened so fast."

"No, no, Miguel. I'm fine. It's just the excitement I'm sure."

A worker yelled for Miguel to consult on how something was to be set up, and I shivered again. I hadn't felt this since just before the accident, and I had that terrible numbness in the pit of my stomach. I shook my body free of it and went to find the girls, who had returned from town with their dresses and new hairdos. I stamped my foot down hard on the ground, determined nothing was going to spoil this fiesta and beautiful wedding.

After my husband had died, I thought I would never find love again, but here it was and so much more—a beautiful new sister-in-law, two lovely homes, and many new friends to complete my life. Miguel had told me he felt the same. Many years ago, when his wife died giving birth to their stillborn son, he had thought his life would be lived alone. Nothing would spoil our second chance, I'd see to that.

With a smile on my face, I went in the house and found laughter, excitement, and all the joy returning to my body and the chill turning to warmth. Hearing a car come to a stop, I glanced out the door to see Miguel and SOS, as we now laughingly called Stefano, deep in conversation. Happy that he had been able to schedule his vacation to be able to attend, I jogged down the drive to welcome him.

"Oh, Stefano, I am so happy you could come. It means the world to me that you are here for our wedding."

"I'm glad to be here, but I'm afraid a few more places must be set as I wasn't able to get here by myself. I have with me several coworkers who had to accompany me, as we are flying out as soon as the fiesta is over."

"Stefano, in this huge gathering, a couple more won't make a difference. Please don't think that. How many are with you?"

"There are eight of us, five men and three women. We are on a new assignment and don't have much time."

"I'm sure eight more is not going to make a difference. There are two pigs roasting in pits, many chickens plucked and on the spits. Are they all IMPACT agents too, Stefano, working for you?"

Shuffling his feet, he answered, looking down, "No, Sue, two of the women and three of the men are FBI agents, and we really are working with them, not the other way around."

That surprised me. "Gosh, you must be on an important case. You must tell us all about it."

"I'm afraid I can't tell you anything right now, Susan, but soon I'll fill you and Miguel in."

"Marvellous! Now I must run and make sure Maria and staff see to your table settings."

The chill returned as I walked toward the caterers, and after I finished my talk with them, I returned to the house. Miguel entered the room and asked Maria and me to accompany him to his office. After having us sit with a glass of wine, he asked if all was ready for the wedding. Maria answered, "Of course, Miguel, we accomplished everything. We knew the fiesta would run long into the night, so we didn't want to leave the preparations for tomorrow morning. After a late night with tequila and wine flowing, and dancing up a storm, I thought everyone would want to sleep in for a while before the wedding. Why?"

Miguel looked annoyed but answered, "Sorrentino brought news with him. The brake line in my car was cut. It was not an accident. As soon as he knew, he started an investigation. At first the agency thought someone was trying to take over Pablo's control of the drug ring, but that didn't make sense. They have since learned that Pablo has a sixteen-year-old son who didn't know about his father's illegal business. He blames us in his grief for his father's death. Stefano thinks he may try again to hurt us at the wedding. With Stefano's help, the wedding will be performed first. Then they can leave in the morning after the fiesta. The agents must get back and can stay no longer. It is a favour to us, protection for such a public event. This is a lot to ask, Susan. I'm sorry. He suggested it was a better plan, as the fiesta can be our wedding reception. What do you think? Want to be my wife a day early?"

I jumped into his arms, holding him close, my head on his shoulder. "Yes, I do! I thought about having it this way but didn't want to upset the apple cart, as everything seemed to be going along so fine. I'll go talk to the girls. They are all down in Cassy's room. There is no reason to tell anyone else about this. Well, you should tell Hugo," I answered as I flew out and ran down the hall.

What a marvellous change of plans, and I was so thankful that Maria had made everyone get ready today instead of getting up at the crack of dawn to accomplish everything. The girls' hair would be in better shape, not having been slept on, and it was just a matter of changing the order of how we dressed. Both outfits were hanging in our rooms, ready to don. Prin was groomed, brushed, and puffed with flowers in her topknot and likely wouldn't look as beautiful tomorrow as she did right now.

Maria knocked and entered my room. "Chica, is this change of plan really all right with you and the girls?"

"Yes, Maria, it really is. In fact everyone is pleased that the wedding will be first." I smiled. "They were all worried their hair would get messed in bed and their flowers look less fresh! All of them are so excited and glad about the change. What time will it be arranged for?"

Maria looked at her watch. "Word is going out as we speak. The chapel service is set for six, the same time the fiesta was to start. It will be immediately after the service now. That will give you time to dress. Miguel is talking to the men now in the dining area. Your son will walk you down after the girls enter, Francisco will carry the rings, and I will stand with Miguel and his friends. I think we have thought of everyone. It should go as planned."

"Maria, if you are so sure everything is set up and going as planned, why are you wringing your hands and your forehead furrowed with worry?"

She startled, stood straight, and dropped her arms. "It's just big sister nerves, my dear. I feel like a mother right now. The news that the accident was an attempt to hurt or kill you and Miguel has come as a shock, and I can't stop thinking about how easily that distraught teen could get close to you both in such a large crowd."

"You are not old enough to be the mother of Miguel or me, but I understand how you feel. The news is a blow. I feel sorry for the boy. With the agents here to help keep an eye out, I feel better. It isn't like he is a hardened criminal, just a young, distraught boy. Maybe knowing he caused the accident and our injuries took the spark of revenge out of him. Okay, we must start dressing and get this show on the road! We have a couple of hours only to do makeup and act silly together. I don't want Cassy, the girls, Joan, and Edward to be upset or miss all the fun."

We decided to split into two rooms to allow more room for dressing and using the mirrors, but there still was a lot of running back and forth. Laughter filled the hallway and jests of "sit still," "I just got mascara on your face," "I can't see my lips," and "move over, silly." It was wonderful having so many friends and family here enjoying each other, laughing and joking together. It made the necessity of bringing everyone together quickly under the circumstances bearable.

Looking down at the diamond-studded watch Miguel had given me as his wedding present, I saw that six o'clock was almost here. I glanced in the full-length mirror, seeing the handmade lace gown curving down my body and gently fluttering in the breeze from the ceiling fan. It was made for me. I placed the diamond comb on my uplifted, bright red, curly hair, and the veil swirled to the floor. I'm sure I felt Miguel's grandmother smile down on my reflection. I was alone in my room, waiting for my son, Edward, whom I was so proud of, to walk me down the aisle.

The girls hadn't understood why I insisted on being alone to dress. A new life for me was beginning, and I wanted to welcome it alone for just a bit of time.

I could hear soft guitar music mingling with Spanish and English chatter as the folks collected in the garden below my window. Like the love I carried inside me, a mixture of Spanish and English. A true miracle at my age. I knelt by the chest that held Miguel's mother's and grandmother's memories. I prayed I would love this good man my entire life, my health and age not hindering our chance for a long and happy life.

I touched my miracle dress, letting the love of the lace fill my fingers, and corrected the fall of my veil. I picked up a single white calla lily to carry and opened the door at the first sound of my son's knock.

"Mum, you ready?"

"Oh yes, honey, I'm ready!"

Chapter 22

The Service

I stood at the rear of the charming old chapel, behind the girls, and lovingly watched my daughter and friends do the one-and-a-half step down the aisle toward the altar. I could see Miguel, Maria, Hugo, and Francisco standing there to the right as the girls moved to the left. *God, how handsome he is*, I thought. Then I placed my hand on my son's arm, and we entered. Everyone was standing and staring at us, and I could hear the oohs and aahs I had known this striking dress would bring.

My son placed my hand into the outstretched hand of the man I would now take as my husband. We gazed into each other's eyes as we delivered the vows we had written. Francisco passed us each a ring. As nervous as he was, he managed to do so without dropping one. I heard the words, "I now pronounce you husband and wife," and then loud clapping and cheering as the bells in the chapel tower rang loudly, trying to outdo the people's cheers.

Miguel and I walked down the aisle to the doors with everyone else trailing behind. Two FBI agents opened them and stood outside observing the crowd. They motioned us out. I glanced up at Miguel with a questioning look, but he patted my hand and did not look down at me. When I stepped out, I realized we would not have to perform the wedding service again, as I remembered a camera and microphones had been in the chapel. I looked over to the side of the building and saw a huge screen and knew that everyone had viewed the service outside.

"Oh, Miguel, that was a wonderful idea. Why didn't I know you had planned that?"

"I didn't, my dear. Stefano brought all the equipment, and his men set it up."

"But—"

I didn't get a chance to finish my sentence as a female agent gently took us by the arm and led us to the arch. Hugo stood at the arch with a microphone and announced in both Spanish and English, "May I introduce Señora and Doctor Miguel Alfonso Cortez Anaya! For a short time, photos may be taken before the food is served. The music will start now. Dance, sing, eat, and make celebration for our dear friends."

Miguel and I stood in the centre of the arch with the men beside Miguel, and the women next to me. Cameras were clicking and clicking. Chants started of "*beso, beso, beso.*" When we turned to kiss, I whispered in his ear, "I feel like a princess."

He turned to look down at me. "You are."

With a great shout of happiness, Miguel picked me up, swinging me around in circles, tears running down his cheeks. The chant started again, "Beso, beso, beso." We gladly complied and kissed deeply.

He stood me on my feet again, and we turned to the crowd below us. Holding hands, we raised them in the air.

That was when the first shot rang out.

There was a moment of silence and stillness, and then everyone seemed to scream at the same time, running in all directions to look for cover but not knowing where to go.

A second shot rang out, and the calla lily in my hand went flying through the air. I felt no pain but saw blood as Miguel threw me to the ground and lay on top of me.

"Miguel, Miguel, get off me," I screamed.

I saw Sorrentino and another man lift Miguel off of me. Blood stained his shirt. I screamed and passed out.

I opened my eyes to see Maria, Cassy, and Edward looking down on me with tears streaking their faces. "Where is Miguel? What the hell happened?" Then it came to me: blood. "No, no, please dear God, no."

Maria held me in her arms. "My dearest Susan, listen to me. The blood is from your hand, which took the bullet. Miguel is fine, just shaken. He is with the agents and Sorrentino; they have the boy in custody. They suspected he was here somewhere and were keeping an eye out for him. Your sister, Joan, is resting, and the girls are talking to and settling down the guests."

I looked down at the hand that had held the beautiful lily and saw only a white bandage. The memory of it flying out of my hand and Miguel diving on top of me came back, and I heard the next shot.

"He covered my body to save me. That was meant for me. Why don't I feel any pain?"

Maria explained that after the shot, I had fainted, and she had given me an injection of painkiller and stitched my wound. "There is no permanent damage to your hand. The bullet went through the soft tissue between your thumb and forefinger. You'll have to wear a bandage for a few days."

Cassy changed places with Maria and held me. Maria returned with an injection of tranquilizer. When I saw the needle, I screamed.

"No, no, the fiesta. I don't want to be knocked out." I wrapped my arms around my body in protest. "The fiesta will continue. Nothing, absolutely nothing is going to spoil our wedding."

If I hadn't been so upset, I would have cracked up laughing at the look of astonishment on their faces.

I sat up. "All right, I want to hear it. What happened? Tell me everything. Get Stefano in here."

As Stefano started to explain, I realized I had known something was wrong the moment I saw him, the moment I had felt the goose bumps and had the chills.

"As I told you, the car losing its brakes was not an accident, Susan. As soon as I knew, I got the team together and came right here. I had no idea what was going to happen, just felt that your lives were in danger. I had no idea he would act so soon or violently. We were just covering you until after the wedding. The sixteen-year-old son of Pablo Diaz blamed you for the death of his father. He is responsible for the accident and the shooting. He is in custody and admitted he was shooting at you but didn't want to kill you, just hurt you. I believe he is an expert shot. He shot your hand and was aiming for your other hand when Miguel threw himself on you, to protect you, causing the boy to miss."

"Good Lord in heaven, what a terrible thing I started. I just should have let the damn drugs into the country and minded my own business. I'm sorry for the boy."

"Sue, don't think that way. You and your friends saved thousands of lives."

"Has everyone left? I don't hear the music or any noise. I expect they were all scared to death and went back to their homes. I wanted the fiesta to go on. I wanted a perfect wedding day. How silly I am."

"Come to window, Susan, and see what the people are doing."

I followed Maria to the window and looked out to where our lovely fiesta would have been held. I was amazed. Everything was still set up perfectly, and between the flower beds, tables, walkways, and chairs, all the guests were kneeling with clasped hands.

"Maria, what are they doing?"

She smiled at me. "Sue, they are showing their love and respect for you and Miguel. They kneel in prayer waiting to hear you are well and will recover."

"Then what are we doing here? Is the dress ruined?" I asked suddenly, realizing I wasn't completely dressed.

"Not one speck of blood on your wedding dress. Only Miguel's shirt got splattered when he fell onto you."

Maria rose, went to the settee, and passed me my miracle dress. I really believed their grandmother had more than just smiled down on my reflection; she also had protected me, sending cold chills and goose bumps to warn me of danger. I held it close to my heart and prayed a thank you.

"Marvellous; now we'll collect Miguel and everyone and get on with this fiesta. Maria, send someone to announce that there will be a fiesta in a few hours and to start the mariachi now and serve the tequila! I just need to lie down and relax until this drug wears off. I also need time to talk more to Sorrentino and Miguel. Then we can get this show on the road again. We've got a celebration to finish!"

Chapter 23

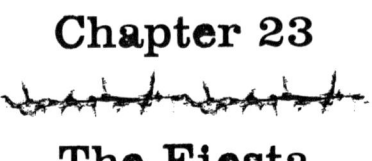

The Fiesta

When I woke from my nap, I found the drug had worn off. I could hear the music, laughter, and chattering of many people talking at the same time in Spanish and English. The fiesta was in full swing.

I quickly washed up, swallowed a Tylenol, and opted for a pair of white slacks and sweater. Better for the cooler evenings and dance than my dream wedding dress. I ran back to the dresser and found a white silk scarf shot with silver to toss around my neck. I applied a little lipstick, and when I checked in the mirror, I looked like a bride—even without the dress. Then again, maybe that was the glow on my cheeks from happiness and love and not my outfit.

I jogged down the hallway and out to the garden. What a sight! There were at least two hundred people dancing, eating, drinking, and talking. The music was loud enough to override the laughter, but it didn't. Children were assembled around brightly coloured papier-mâché piñatas. Each took a turn, blindfolded, whacking them, trying to break the clay pot inside that was filled with treats, sweets, and surprises. When the piñata was broken, all the treats scattered over the ground and the children groped for them, each trying to get the most.

Everyone was dancing—boys with their mothers, girls with their fathers. Babies were being held high in the air and jiggled to the rhythm of the music. As fiestas went, this definitely rated a ten.

Table after table was covered with food and drinks. Tortillas were being made by hand beside the *al pastor* spit stand. The barbecues were white hot with racks of beef sizzling, ready to fill a tortilla. The pigs were out of the pits, carved, and sitting beside the clay pots of beans, salsas, and salads. I knew there were tables somewhere holding platters of sweets, including Mexican wedding cakes and flans. I also knew there would be an outrageous wedding cake with eight or ten layers, each leading up a staircase that would hold the figurine I had chosen for the top. Large enough to feed the crowd, it would take up a whole banquet table.

Finally I spotted Maria and Miguel by the fountain talking to some townsfolk I didn't know. Miguel felt my eyes on him and turned to smile. With outstretched arms, he quickly approached.

"Thank heaven you are awake and, by the look of you, feel as good as you look. That was a wise decision, Sue, to wear slacks and sweater." He said this as his eyes moved up and down the length of my body. "You look like a bride."

"I should hope so, Miguel. I am a bride." I smiled up into the face I so loved. Miguel grabbed my arm. "Come on, honey, they are waiting to see us for the first time dance as a married couple."

"Good heavens, I'm starving. Can't I eat first?" I asked as I skipped along behind him.

"Nope, dance, drink the toast, and then I'll let you eat," Miguel answered.

"Oh, so that's the way our married life is to be? You give the orders, right down to the time I'm to eat?" I joked back.

The people separated as we reached the dance floor, making it our personal space. The music changed to a waltz, and as Miguel led me in the first dance, I glided to the music with closed eyes.

Late into the morning, people drifted away, back to their homes or rooms. Miguel picked me up in his arms as though I was light as a feather and walked with me to our room. I went with the flow and closed my eyes to float toward the love that waited for me behind the closed door of our suite.

We only had a few days at the ranch before we left to honeymoon in Canada. Miguel was excited about being in the snow for the first time and had studied the brochures for Banff National Park again and again before deciding on the condo he'd rent. I had seen the photos and ads for many but tried not to influence his decision. As soon as he saw the photo of the condo with a fireplace and an honest-to-god polar bearskin rug in front of it, his mind couldn't have been changed. He outlandishly teased me about what he had in mind for us on that rug.

We planned on visiting Victoria on the west coast, Halifax on the east side, and Ottawa in the middle—meeting with friends and family, seeing their homes—but Banff was our main destination. Getting off the plane in Calgary, Miguel was a sight to see. He shivered dramatically until we were snug in our warm chalet.

"Dear me," Miguel said, "I'm not so sure now this was such a good idea. I wanted to see snow, but I'm freezing to death, and we're not near a ski hill yet."

"Oh, for heaven's sake, hon, stop being a baby." I laughed at him as he curled up in a chair, wrapping the bedspread around his shoulders.

"Once we get you a heavier jacket, warmer socks, and boots, you'll be fine. You shouldn't have insisted on wearing that suit. A dress shirt isn't the warmest thing you could have worn. You just wanted to look handsome for the stewardess," I said, still laughing.

"Well, I'm calling room service for a drink and hot coffee, and also a clothing store to have some things delivered. I'm not going out again dressed like this," he said through chattering teeth.

The bearskin rug was forgotten.

The next morning, Miguel was eager to venture out to look for snow. Dressed warmly, wearing twice as much clothing as anyone else at the resort, he appeared twenty pounds heavier.

"Miguel, you'll have to wear just the ski suit and boots this afternoon when we go for your lessons," I warned him with a squint.

"I know, and I will. I'll get used to it quickly, and moving around will help."

His lesson that first day went great, and he got through it without one broken or sprained limb. I was very proud of Miguel and took a hundred photos of him making snow angels and a snowman. He thought snowball fights were terrific and really enjoyed them more each time; his aim was true and he smashed me with a snowball.

That night, the poor polar bear skin rug had a workout and the woodpile went down two feet.

Before we knew it, our time in Canada was up. As much fun and enjoyment as we had, we knew it was time to head for home.

Chapter 24

Two Years Later

Francisco stood proudly as he received his diploma. He turned and smiled down on Miguel, Maria, and me. How proud we were of his accomplishments. He had excelled at secondary school, and with our tutoring, had skipped several grades. He was excited about next year and attending the four years of prep classes that would ready him for university and then medical school. His decision to study pharmaceuticals and medicine had never wavered, and we knew it was because of his experiences with the counterfeiters.

Internet sales for cheap drugs had increased alarmingly since the economy had dropped. Every penny counted, and folks were doing what they could. Sorrentino was working relentlessly and would be attending the upcoming Asia-Pacific Economic Cooperation (APEC) summit.

Online sales were now a global concern. The United States, Australia, and Canada pioneered Operation Pangea. Since 2011, ninety-nine countries had successfully shut down more than thirteen thousand websites and confiscated illicit and fake pills worth $36 million. They discovered over 721 types of fake drugs.

Sorrentino had kept us informed, and we shared that knowledge with Francisco. He was determined to study and be of help with this enormous problem that nearly took our lives when we stupidly thought we could fight these crime lords.

We had been lucky to get away with all our lives intact. Our amateurish actions and daring could have brought more disaster.

Our lives continued to be calm and content after the fiesta and our honeymoon in Canada. I made sure Miguel holidayed during the winter so he could learn to ski, but that was an excuse. I wanted him to freeze his ass off and understand why so many Canadians came to Mexico for the sun and warmth. It worked too! He couldn't believe people would exist with seven months of below-zero temperatures and snow to shovel, although he did get to be quite good on the slopes.

Our time was spent at the clinics and time off at the ranch. I valued having the extra rooms at the ranch so our friends and Cassy, Steve, Edward, and May could visit whenever they wanted. I enjoyed and loved my children so very much. It was with deep regret that I realized my sister Joan was not well enough to make the trip each year, but the times she had made it down were filled with such joy. Each day held Kodak moments, and we had recorded each one, filling many albums. Our days had been full of love and happiness.

I returned to college for part-time classes and now worked as an assistant in the clinics. I loved working with Miguel and Maria. She was a true friend and sister to me. My only sorrow was she had not found her true love with whom to share her life and happiness.

Many blissful fiestas were held for birthdays, weddings, and parties for friends. Chun Lee, his family, Hugo, Syl, and Nancy were always close by and visited often. Francisco stayed in touch with all his friends. Ricki now managed several banana boats purchased from his share of the reward; Toni and Chui had a charming restaurant, named Explosion; and Sonya and Patti each were managing one of the clinics to free up time for Miguel and Maria. They had all used their rewards well.

We certainly acted irrationally, but we had accomplished what we set out to do. We all stayed extremely close friends and got together as often as we could.

Funny, though, now that I think of it, we never discussed that night. I'm sure it was in the back of our minds each time we got together, but the subject never was mentioned.

I smiled up at Miguel and received a wink in return. We were so close; he knew exactly where my mind had wandered. He reached for my hand, and we smiled into each other's eyes before returning our gaze to the stage and sharing our wink with Francisco.

He could hardly stand still, eager to get to the ranch, thinking only of the fiesta arranged for his friends and their parents to celebrate graduation and walk into high school. He was tall, slender, strong, and handsome. God had certainly sent us a treasure for our son.

I remembered Francisco saying the first night we met, "I live in dump, find good treasures. I smart."

I didn't know then just how right he had been. Not only he, but also I, had found my treasure in the dump, my beautiful, smart treasure, Rat.

We had some dangerous beginnings but now a loving and blessed end.

A chill ran down my arms. Every hair stood on end. I shivered in the hot noonday sun as goose bumps stood out over my body. I looked toward the sky and whispered, "Oh God, not again! What now?"

Miguel smiled at me, saying, "Chica, you should have brought a wrap! The winter winds have started to blow. I can feel the chill in the evening breeze; you must too."

I glanced up and answered, "Yes, Miguel, I should have. I do feel the chill in the air." But I was thinking, *I hope it was only the cool evening breeze.*

Author's Note:

This is the end of the novel but hopefully the beginning of your quest to help educate yourself and aid in the fight to end this atrociously inconspicuous and unpublicized growing crime.

My motivation in writing this novel was to bring to your attention the volume of the counterfeit pharmaceutical drug trade and the dangers that can transpire from not being aware. I wanted to present the facts in an interesting and entertaining story without the statistics being boring. Listed on the next page, you will find resources to continue your education of this horrific criminal activity and the difficulty federal agencies in nearly one hundred countries have in trying to stop this extremely profitable criminal activity. Learn to protect yourself and your children, family, and friends. This is a global concern. Do what you can to halt the death and illness of thousands every year. I hope you have enjoyed the characters Susan and Rat and their presentation in bringing the facts and problem to you. Search "counterfeit pharmaceutical drugs" and "Operation Pangea VI" for more information. Educate yourself; knowledge is the weapon you can use to help bring down this crime.

Resources

http://www.interpol.int/News-and-media/News/2013/PR077

What are counterfeit medicines?
According to the WHO definition, a counterfeit medicine is one "which is deliberately and fraudulently mislabelled with respect to identity and/or source. Counterfeiting can apply to both branded and generic products, and counterfeit products may include products with the correct ingredients or with the wrong ingredients, without active ingredients, with insufficient active ingredients or with fake packaging."

Pangea VI
The operation has gained significant momentum since its launch in 2008. The first phase of the operation brought together ten countries; a number that has now risen to around one hundred.

Dates: 18–28 June 2013
Participating countries: ninety-nine in total
Results:
- **10.1 million illicit and counterfeit pills confiscated**
- **Estimated value: US$36 million**
- **More than 13,700 websites shut down**
- **Some 534,00 packages inspected by regulators and customs authorities, of which around 41,000 were confiscated**
- **Some 213 individuals are currently under investigation or under arrest for a range of offences, including illegal Internet activity.**

In Canada in 2014, the Royal Canadian Mounted Police (RCMP) and Canada Border Services Agency (CBSA) joined forces with Interpol to inspect 3,444 packages originating in nineteen countries. Of these, 3,223 packages, which contained 238,820 illicit and fake medicines at a street value of C$1,032,514, have been seized.

CPSIA information can be obtained at www.ICGtesting.com
Printed in the USA
BVOW04s0644141014

370647BV00001B/1/P